Hear the Wind Blow

Hear the Wind Blow

AMERICAN FOLK SONGS RETOLD

by Scott R. Sanders

Illustrations by Ponder Goembel

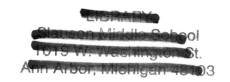
BRADBURY PRESS   NEW YORK

Bradbury Press
An Affiliate of Macmillan, Inc.
866 Third Avenue, New York, N.Y. 10022
Collier Macmillan Canada, Inc.
Manufactured in the United States of America
1   3   5   7   9   10   8   6   4   2

The text of this book is set in 14 pt. Caslon Old Face No. 2.
The illustrations are black and white pencil and ink drawings
reproduced in halftone.
Designed by Mina Greenstein

Library of Congress Cataloging in Publication Data:
Sanders, Scott R. (Scott Russell), 1945-   Hear the wind blow.
Summary: Twenty tales taken from folksongs reflecting American
history, e.g. "Yankee Doodle," "John Henry," "The Blue-Tail
Fly," and "Frankie and Johnny." Includes the original
folk song lyrics.
1. Short stories, American. 2. Folk-songs, English—United
States. [1. Short stories. 2. Folk songs, American]
I. Goembel, Ponder, ill. II. Title.
PZ7.S19786He   1985   [Fic]   85-4160
ISBN 0-02-778140-2

TO JESSE AND EVA
my two favorite reasons
for singing songs
and telling stories

Foreword

LONG BEFORE I was old enough to read, I knew this lonesome tune:

> *Down in the valley,*
> *The valley so low,*
> *Hang your head over,*
> *Hear the wind blow.*

The valley I imagined was the one behind my house in Tennessee, and the head weighted down with loneliness was my own head, and the wind I heard was the same one that swayed the hickory tree outside my bedroom window. Now, many years later, in quiet moments, I still hear that wind blowing.

Certain songs haunt us, loop and loop through the mind, sometimes because of their melodies, sometimes because of the stories they tell. Once we hear about the dying cowboy who gives instructions for his funeral, or the frog who courts a mouse, or the gal who shoots her two-timing man, or the farmer's wife who gets carried off by the Devil, or the train engineer who races against the clock—once we hear about such folk in songs, we are not likely to forget them. Often their stories come through only in bits and pieces—a vivid scene, a hint of quirky character—yet even in such bright fragments they lay hold of the imagination.

In this book I have told my own versions of the stories from twenty American folk songs. Some of the originals are famous—"Yankee Doodle," "John Henry," "Frankie and Johnny"—while others are less well known—tall tales, courtship ditties, sea chanteys. They range in time from the period of American settlement, up through the Revolution and the Civil War, into our own century. There are wilderness songs and city songs, songs about slaves and buffalo hunters, outlaws and cowboys, whales and wars, tragic songs and comic ones. What they have in common is durability. They have stayed in the memories of people in this land for generations. Together they chart a rough history of America, the westward searching from the Atlantic to the Pacific.

Anyone who compares my tales with the lyrics will see that I have often traveled a long way from the original. A line here or an image there would set me wondering, the way lights glimpsed away off at night through the darkness will stir up thoughts. Sometimes I tried to imagine what led to the events described in the song, or I invented details the singer never gave us, or I filled in the mysterious gaps in a plot. My tales are not meant to rival or replace the songs, which burn with their own fire, but rather to give a storyteller's response to the human stuff that inspired the singer. When I listen to the wind blowing, I hear voices. In these pages I set down some of the tales the wind has brought me.

S.R.S.
April 1985

Contents

Hear the Wind Blow

When I First Came to This Land

[TRADITIONAL]

When I first came to this land
I was not a wealthy man.
So I got myself a shack,
And I did what I could.

And I called my shack, "Break-My-Back."
But the land was sweet and good,
And I did what I could.

When I first came to this land
I was not a wealthy man.
So I got myself a cow,
And I did what I could.

And I called my cow, "No-Milk-Now,"
Called my shack, "Break-My-Back."
But the land was sweet and good,
And I did what I could.

When I first came to this land
I was not a wealthy man.
So I got myself a duck,
And I did what I could.

And I called my duck, "Out-of-Luck,"
Called my cow, "No-Milk-Now,"
Called my shack, "Break-My-Back."
But the land was sweet and good,
And I did what I could.

When I first came to this land
I was not a wealthy man.
So I got myself a wife,
And I did what I could.

And I called my wife, "Run-for-Your-Life,"
Called my duck, "Out-of-Luck,"
Called my cow, "No-Milk-Now,"
Called my shack, "Break-My-Back."
But the land was sweet and good,
And I did what I could.

When I first came to this land
I was not a wealthy man.
So I got myself a daughter,
And I did what I could.

And I called my daughter, "Run-Fetch-Water,"
Called my wife, "Run-for-Your-Life,"
Called my duck, "Out-of-Luck,"
Called my cow, "No-Milk-Now,"
Called my shack, "Break-My-Back."
But the land was sweet and good,
And I did what I could.

When I first came to this land
I was not a wealthy man.
So I got myself a son,
And I did what I could.

And I called my son, "My-Work's-Done,"
Called my daughter, "Run-Fetch-Water,"
Called my wife, "Run-for-Your-Life,"
Called my duck, "Out-of-Luck,"
Called my cow, "No-Milk-Now,"
Called my shack, "Break-My-Back."
But the land was sweet and good,
And I did what I could.

Skinny Uncle Swan, who barely cast a shadow, sailed off to America in search of his fortune. The wind that drove him away from Sweden blew straight down across the North Pole. Sea gulls flew in tight flocks to keep warm. Too young to go along, Christer shivered on the pier in Stockholm and watched his uncle's ship until the edge of the sea shut behind it like a door. America! thought Christer. Country of the sun, he thought, land of Indians and riches and bears!

After seven years Uncle Swan returned home to Sweden as fat as an Easter goose. The buttons of his vest would no longer meet the buttonholes. It was true he still wore the same old vest, which had taken on the color of bacon grease. And he still wore his old top hat, which had come to resemble a hornet's nest. But his belly was bulging, and so was the wallet he drew from the pocket of his tattered coat. He opened the wallet just far enough to give Christer's family a peep inside, and what should they see but a glint of gold! Dazzled, they agreed that his ratty coat and greasy vest and cockeyed hat were no more than a tramp's disguise. "Don't look at his poor-man's clothes," said Christer's father, "look at his rich-man's belly."

Soon he would buy himself a Swedish island, Uncle Swan announced, he would fill the trees with blue canaries, build himself a palace of marble with bathtubs of silver, and get himself a nice round princess for a wife. But first he would have to rest up from his travels. Day after day he sat by the fire, smoking a pipe, eating soup, spitting now and again into a brass bowl, all the while describing the wonders of America. Christer forgot his chores, forgot his girlfriends with their braided hair, nearly forgot to breathe, he was so absorbed in listening.

In the rivers of America, said Uncle Swan, the fish jostle one another for room to swim; you can snatch them up with your bare hands. Turkeys wander into your cabin and climb onto your chopping block. To make wine in America, you need only place tubs beneath a wild grapevine and wait for the fruit to burst from the fullness of its own juices. Maple sap is syrupy enough to flavor your tea. Land is so cheap you can buy a plantation with a handful of coins. The soil is potent. Uncut, the trees there die of old age. Any night you can hear the old ones crashing down under their own weight. The winters are mild. The rains are hard and short, and fall only in late afternoon, to leave the days clear for sun.

"But what of the English? Don't they occupy all the land?" said Christer's father.

"They're timid," Uncle Swan replied. "They fear the deep forests and stay in their brick towns along the coast."

"And what of the savages? Aren't they troublesome?" said Christer's mother.

"They run from the ring of an ax. The few who stay behind will trade you a wagonload of beaver skins for a copper thimble."

"If America is such a land of plenty," Christer's father demanded, "why, pray tell, did you come back?"

A mist like fine cobwebs settled over Uncle Swan's eyes. "Reasons of the heart," was all he would say.

Before long Christer's father grew tired of giving Uncle

Swan doses of tobacco. Christer's mother grew tired of feeding him. "If he wishes to keep that walrus belly," she said, "let him open his pouch and show us this famous gold. Let us see to the bottom of his fat wallet."

Soon only Christer sat with his uncle at the fire or walked beside him along the bird-filled river, listening to the tales of America after the others had turned away with shrugs of boredom. Now and again he asked a question—about the Indians or the bears, perhaps—but he refused to pester Uncle Swan about the mysterious wallet. Grown to be a young man, his heart as pierced with shadowy inlets as the coastline of Sweden, Christer knew the sweetness of secrets. The last way to get a peek into Uncle Swan's dark pouch, he imagined, was to beg for one. So he kept mum about the wallet.

One rainy day Uncle Swan tiptoed into Christer's room and whispered, "Don't you want to see what prizes I brought back from America?"

"Oh," said Christer, hiding his eagerness, "I suppose it's only gold."

"Rarer than gold!"

Christer shrugged. "I guess I might as well have a look."

Whereupon Uncle Swan plumped himself down on the bed, opened the pouch, and began hauling out his treasures and laying them one by one on the eiderdown. Instead of gold, out came a musket ball with a crease in it, a blue feather, a bone carved in the shape of a spoon, a flint arrowhead, a copper hatpin, a whorled seashell, a chip of wine-colored wood, and then lock after lock of hair. Each lock was tied in a bundle with silken thread.

"Uncle Swan!" breathed Christer. "Did you have so many sweethearts?"

"The gray hair is from a wolf I killed," said Uncle Swan, "the black from a bear, the brown from a badger, the cinnamon curl from a buffalo. How do you suppose I grew so fat? It was from eating all these beasts!"

"But what about this pale ringlet," said Christer, holding up a lock the color of moonbeams, "surely this one belonged to a sweetheart?"

"No, no, that's from the ear of a mountain lion."

"And this red tuft?"

"That's from the tail of a fox."

"And this snowy curl?"

"Sliced from a wild goat's beard."

"Not a single woman gave you a snippet of her hair?"

The mist like fine cobwebs settled again over Uncle Swan's eyes. "The truth is, my lad, I was frightened out of my wits by those women in America."

"They wouldn't frighten me!" said Christer.

"Are you sure?"

"As sure as I'm standing here!"

"Then take this coin," said Uncle Swan, drawing the solitary gold piece from the bottom of his wallet, "and buy yourself passage to America. But whatever you do, don't let your parents know you're going."

Secretly, Christer boarded a ship and sailed away from Sweden on a morning when the wind blew straight across the North Pole. He took with him an ax, a musket, a shovel, a sack of wheat for planting, and a silver ring to give to the woman he would choose for his sweetheart. To keep warm he rubbed together three pennies, which were all he had left from Uncle Swan's gold piece.

When he landed in Philadelphia he discovered that for three pennies he could not buy even a roll to eat or a bed for the night. So he tied his gear to his back and trudged westward into the wilds of Pennsylvania.

In the mountains he came upon a man who offered to sell him, for one penny, a shack that was so full of holes you could hardly tell when you were inside and when you were out. Christer paid over his coin and moved in. Now I have myself a shack, he thought. I'm halfway to a farm. But he might just as well have been living in a tree. The wind wailed through the gaps in the wall with the voices of drowning animals. Wind whipped shingles from the roof and drove smoke through holes in the chimney. Rain fell not only at dusk, as Uncle Swan had promised, but at any hour of the day or night, and the roof leaked around the clock.

All of this got Christer's dander up. He wouldn't let the weather make fun of his shack that way, not while he had two hands and a strong back. So for seven weeks he worked like a demon. He propped up the rafters with poles, chopped fresh logs for the walls, stuffed moss in the cracks, smeared pine tar on the puncheon floor, mended the chimney with clay, dipped his linen handkerchief in grease and plastered it over the lone window. When he had finished, the shack was as tight and trim as a music box, but Christer himself was worn down to a frazzle. Over the front door he hung a sign that read: Break-My-Back.

He was still resting up when along came an old woman driving a skin-and-bones cow. "For one penny," she muttered, "I would gladly sell this wretched beast and never look at her bony backside again."

Christer paid over a penny and tied the cow to a stake in front of his shack. Now he was a farmer indeed, he thought. When he tried milking the cow, however, she would not give a drop. He pulled armfuls of sweet grass for her, lugged buckets of water from the spring, scratched her ears and brushed her piebald fur, but nothing came out of her except moans. Thinking she might not like standing in the rain, Christer moved her inside the shack and tied her to the leg of his bed. Now she gave moos instead of moans, but still not a drop to drink. So in disgust he carved on one of her horns the name No-Milk-Now.

By and by, an Indian came to the door and offered to sell him a freshly shot duck. One penny, said the Indian. The arrow still dangled from the bird's belly. Roast duck! thought Christer, as he paid over his last coin. No sooner had the Indian pulled out his arrow and slipped away into the woods, however, than the duck began hopping and scuttling across the floor of the shack. Christer chased it around and around the bed, around the cow, around the table, and finally caught it by the tail feathers. The eyes it turned on him were so brown and pitiful that Christer could not bring himself to wring its neck. So he rubbed salve on its wound. He made up a box for it in one corner and on the side, with a cinder from the fireplace, wrote the duck's name: Out-of-Luck.

In the spring Christer dug a garden, planted wheat, then

set off with his musket to hunt for bears. He walked right across the mountain and eventually discovered a cave. "Come on out here, you bear!" he cried. Smoke was leaking from a hole on the slope above the cave. "Bear!" he called again, this time with less confidence. From inside came the noise of pots banging. "Bear?" he called, uncertainly. Next came the voice of a woman yelling in Swedish, and a moment later out walked the woman herself. She was waggling a knife and wearing a bearskin. Before they had exchanged a word, Christer fell in love with her.

"I thought bears lived in this cave," he said.

"Five of them used to," the woman answered, "but I ran three of them off and skinned the other two."

Her name was Helga, and she was so beautiful that Christer was afraid to look straight at her. He might have taken a warning from the fate of the bears; instead he asked her to marry him. She agreed, but not until she had examined his shack, his cow, and his duck. "Not bad for a start," she concluded.

He gave her the silver ring he had brought with him from Sweden. The very minute they were married Helga wrote down a list of the jobs he must do before dark. She wanted a hearth made from river stones, a broom fashioned of horsetails, a sack of fragrant pine needles, and a quart of mushrooms. Christer loved her so much that he finished every single job. The next day the list was longer, and the day after it was longer still.

So things rolled along for months until Christer, wobbly in his joints from all the work, decided to run away. Before he had gone a mile, Helga came charging after, grabbed him by the scruff of the neck, and dragged him home, scolding all the while. The second time he ran away she gave him a good yank on his beard and a warning: "You just try it once more, leaving me defenseless out here in the wilds, and I'll make a rug out of your hide."

Defenseless? thought Christer. He stayed home after that and worked like a donkey. Under his breath he called his wife Run-for-Your-Life, but he never called her that to her face.

In due time a daughter was born, a blond-headed squealer. Now Christer hoped he could take it easy, with a girl to fetch and do. But the daughter took after the mother, and soon the two of them were running him ragged. "Shake a leg and stoke up that fire," they would say. "Why not build a barn for the cow? And how about a pen for the duck while you're at it?" So much talking made the two women thirsty, and they were forever sending Christer on trips to the spring. This led him to call his daughter, in secret, Run-Fetch-Water.

Lord, Lord, thought Christer, why did I ever come to this land?

By and by a son was born, a white-haired little bull of a boy. Christer named him Swan, in honor of his uncle, whom he still loved despite all the trouble Uncle Swan had started with his grand talk of America. Ah, but what was the good of a son? Another mouth to feed, more errands to run. Christer knew better than to look for help from a child. Yet the boy sprouted up, strong and willing. Before long he was cutting firewood and fetching water. Young Swan was so clever that he would finish every job before the mother and daughter could think what to ask him next. They forgot how to holler. Soon the shack was filled with laughter. Christer's hands grew soft from loafing and his belly grew fat from drinking milk and eating roast duck.

So they lived together for years and years on the side of that Pennsylvania mountain, in the shack called Break-My-Back, Christer, along with No-Milk-Now, his cow, and Out-of-Luck, his duck, and Run-for-Your-Life, his wife, and Run-Fetch-Water, his daughter, and the son whom he called My-Work's-Done.

Springfield Mountain

[TRADITIONAL]

On Springfield Mountain there did dwell,
A handsome youth, I knowed him well,
Lieutenant Myrick's only son,
A likely lad of twenty-one.

One summer evening he did go
Up to the meadow for to mow.
He scarce had mowed half round the field
When a poison serpent bit his heel.

When he received his deathly wound
He laid his scythe down on the ground.
To go back home was his intent,
Calling aloud long as he went.

His calls were heard both far and near,
But no friend to him did appear.
They thought it was some workman's call.
Alas, poor man, alone did fall.

Sal took his heel all in her mouth
For to suck the poison out.
Alas she had a rotten tooth,
And so the poison killed them both.

Day being past, night coming on,
The father went to seek his son,
And there he found his only son,
Cold as a stone, dead on the ground.

He took him up and carried him home,
And on the way did lament and mourn,
Saying, "I heard, but did not come,
And now I'm left alone to mourn."

Timothy Myrick was afraid of only two creatures under the sun—his father, and the rattlesnake that lived on Springfield Mountain. The rattler was long enough to curl around the fattest oak in Massachusetts and still nibble on its tail. The father was short, but made up for what he lacked in size with a giant's temper. He was a lieutenant in the king's army, and nothing pleased him more than marching through the woods in search of Indians or helping the tax collector hunt up settlers hiding in the hollows. At home, he always had the look of a man who ate stones for breakfast and sawdust for dinner. He never smiled, never joked, never tickled Timothy with his fingers or his words. From morning until night it was, "Carry in the firewood, boy, water the horses, fork the hay, hoe the weeds."

At least the snake would give a buzz of its tail before striking. Timothy's father struck without warning. He was a moody, broody grump of a man. If the woodbox ran low or the hogs waddled through the split-rail fence, he would pounce on Timothy and give him a spanking. Timothy loved to go barefoot, but if he kicked off his shoes and left them lying in the doorway, the father was sure to trip over them and fling them at his head, shouting, "I'll teach you to pick up your shoes, you good-for-nothing!"

The father was a kettle filled to the brim with meanness. When he boiled over and the anger hissed from his mouth, he would send Timothy to fetch the cows from Springfield Mountain. The boy ran barefoot after the cows through the long snaky grasses, barefoot over the snaky ledges. Was that a buzz he heard? Was it a rattle? His heart thumped like a wildcat in a barrel.

At the age of twenty-one Timothy started growing whiskers. They came in red and thick, like rusty nails. He raked his palm along his jaw and felt a fresh wind of courage blow through him. He would have run away to sea, leaving his father and the rattler behind in Massachusetts, if he hadn't found a sweetheart. Sarah was her name. He called her Sally in a whisper that made her ears turn pink. Her cheeks stayed pink all the time. Sally's hair was the color of corn silk, her eyes shone like dippers of water, and her whistling made the sparrows hush up and listen. Only one flaw kept her from being perfect, and that only showed when she grinned: she had a rotten tooth. Surrounded by healthy teeth, it looked like a burned stump in a field of snow. The blacksmith offered to pull it for her, but she was afraid of his grimy pliers and his bulgy muscles. She was afraid of nothing else under the sun, not even the rattlesnake or Timothy's father, but she trembled at the idea of visiting the blacksmith.

Timothy loved her, teeth and all, and told her so when they went out walking. They walked in the evenings, after his father had run out of chores to give him. As they strolled through the village or beside the river, the last sunlight played abracadabra with shadows. The tricky light made rabbits look like forgotten baskets, and churns look like turkeys.

The only place they never walked was on Springfield Mountain. "I'd rather hop on burning coals than go anywhere near that rattler," said Timothy.

The snake was growing old. His fangs were loose and his scales were slipping like shingles from a mossy roof, but he was still king of the long grasses, still king of the stony ledges.

The father hated to see Timothy and Sally strolling with their elbows hooked together and their heads nearly touching like a pair of cooing pigeons. "What on earth do you find to jabber about?" he demanded. "Jabber, jabber, jabber, for three hours after supper. Don't you have anything better to do than slouch about with a black-toothed girl?"

Timothy did his chores and kept his mouth shut.

Then late one afternoon the father cut himself while sharpening the scythe, and went hopping around the barn, clutching his thumb and yelling blue blazes.

Timothy heard the cries all the way down in the springhouse, where he was fetching water. Father must have got kicked by a horse, he thought, or been crushed under a beam, or fallen into the fireplace, or some such awful thing as that. He ran to the barn for a look.

"What are you gawking at?" the father shouted.

"I wondered if you needed help," Timothy replied.

"Help my foot! You wondered if I'd been killed!"

Timothy stood in the barn door and didn't say a word.

"Well, if you're so itchy to be helpful," said the father, "you can finish sharpening the scythe."

In silence, biting his tongue, Timothy sharpened the scythe on the grindstone.

When the curving blade gleamed in the slant of afternoon sunlight, the father said, "Now you can go and mow the meadow on Springfield Mountain."

Timothy couldn't hold his tongue any longer. "But it's getting on for evening!"

"You can make a start today and finish the mowing tomorrow."

"But Sally will be expecting me to come by!"

"You can sashay with your black-toothed girl another evening."

A shout rose in Timothy's throat, but his father gave him the hard look of a man who'd eaten stones. So Timothy swal-

lowed his anger, took the scythe, and trudged up Springfield Mountain. Long before he reached the meadow, all he could hear was the scuff of his bare feet in the dirt and the rabbity thump of his heart.

At the edge of the mowing field he lifted up his voice to the snake: "Go in your hole, Mr. Rattler, go hide in the dark earth."

With sweeps of the scythe he laid the long wavery grass in rows, row after row, all around the meadow. Every now and again he paused to whet the blade with a stone he carried in his pocket, and he called again to the snake. He listened for the buzz of rattles, but heard only the whisk of stone on blade, the hiss of falling grass, the rush of his blood.

All the while the old rattlesnake, with loose fangs and the scales slipping off its back, lay curled in the grass at the center of the meadow, listening. Timothy swung the blade, row upon row, working toward the shadowy center. When the noise of the cutting drew too near, the snake shook its tail, but the young man never heard. The old snake gave fair warning, then opened his jaws and struck at the grass-stained heel.

The meadow, high on the west slope of the mountain, held the light long after the valley below had filled with the ink of darkness. Sally was down there in the gloom, waiting by her garden gate for Timothy to come by, when she heard his screams. The sound made the hair stiffen on the nape of her neck. She grabbed up her skirts and ran straight toward the wailing. She never looked left, never looked right, but dashed straight up the mountainside to the rattlesnake meadow. The moaning led her to him, a dark shape curled on the ground.

In the last wink of sunlight the only color she could see was the red of his beard and the twin red holes on his swollen heel.

"Don't go!" she cried.

Timothy groaned and twitched, his body on the cold ground, his mind in another field far beyond hearing.

Sally pressed her mouth over the snakebite and sucked at the poison, and the poison found her bad tooth, and through that dark door found its way to her heart.

When Timothy did not come home for supper, and did not come for bedtime, the father began to simmer. What tricks was the boy up to this time? Had he run away to sea? Suppose Timothy and Sally had slipped off to get married?

By morning the father's anger had softened into worry. At first light he went to the meadow on Springfield Mountain, and there he found them, boy and girl, Timothy cradled in Sally's arms, their bodies gone as still as the new-mown grass. One by one the father carried them down, first the girl and then the boy, and all the way going and coming, staggering under the weight, he wept.

Yankee Doodle

[TRADITIONAL]

Yankee Doodle went to town,
Riding on a pony,
He stuck a feather in his cap
And called it Macaroni.

    Yankee Doodle, keep it up,
    Yankee Doodle Dandy,
    Mind the music and the step
    And with the girls be handy!

Father and I went down to camp,
Along with Captain Gooding,
And there we saw both men and boys
As thick as hasty pudding.

There was Captain Washington
Upon a slapping stallion,
Giving orders to his men,
I guess it was a million.

The troopers they would gallop up
And fire right in our faces,
It scared me almost half to death
To see them run such races.

We saw a little barrel, too,
Its head was made of leather,
They knocked on it with little clubs
And called the folks together.

And then we saw a giant gun
Large as a log of maple,
Upon a deuced little cart
A load for father's cattle.

And every time they shoot it off
It takes a horn of powder,
It makes a noise like father's gun,
Only a nation louder.

I can't tell you half I see,
They kept up such a smother,
So I took my hat off, made a bow
And scampered home to mother.

Yankee Doodle is the tune,
Americans delight in,
'Twill do to whistle, sing or play
And just the thing for fightin'.

O ne time in Boston there was a stableboy named Jonathan, but the neighbors called him Doodle because he was such a scamp for playing tricks on strangers. He was a long, gawky fellow, with ears that curved out like soup ladles, one eye that pointed north while the other pointed south, a pig's flabby lips, crooked teeth, and a chin you could have hung a pot on. To look at him, you would have thought his head was filled with lard, he was that simple-seeming.

But Doodle wasn't simple. His mind was like a spider's web, catching the least little tug or breeze. He always slept with one eye open, to see who might be sneaking up on him. From the time he was just a nub of a boy, neighbors found it never paid to look down your nose at him, for if you did he would diddle you and doodle you and tie you in knots. Strangers, who did not know any better, judged Doodle by his looks. When travelers handed over their horses to him, they used small words and talked very loud, figuring him for a blockhead.

One day a British soldier in a coat as red as the shell on a boiled lobster rode up to the stable and shouted at Doodle, "Here, boy! Brush and feed!"

Doodle obliged by hanging a bucket of oats on the saddle horn and reaching up to brush the soldier's coat.

"No, no, you idiot! *I'm* the man and *he's* the horse!" The soldier smacked himself on the chest and the horse on the neck.

Doodle looked from horse to rider, pretending to guess which was which, blinking his meandery eyes.

"Well, can't you *say* anything?" the soldier demanded.

Whereupon Doodle began talking with the horse about the weather and religion and such matters.

The soldier groaned. "No, no, no! Feed *him* and talk with *me!*"

A light of understanding came into Doodle's face. He

tugged his lips into a grin, as if he had just recited the alphabet backward. Then at last he forked some hay and poured water for the horse and asked the man a question about celestial mechanics. The soldier, who had never heard of celestial mechanics, was so foxed and befuddled that he paid Doodle twice the fee and hurried from the stable, muttering about the idiocy of these Yankees.

Now this soldier belonged to an army that had just arrived from England. The king had sent them to put down a revolt among the colonists. For the soldiers it was like a holiday. Imagine these backwoodsmen and shopkeepers standing on their hind legs and barking defiance at the king of England! The soldiers trooped through the streets of Boston in their lobster coats, singing about cannon fire and maidens, jeering at the townspeople who watched from behind curtains.

When a gang of them spied Doodle playing a flute in the door of his stable, they cried, "Why, there's a prize Yankee for you! Look at the puss on him! Has he got enough wits to wipe his nose, do you think? Let's go see if he knows how to talk."

The soldiers crowded up to the stable. Their captain strutted forward, gave them a wink over his shoulder, and demanded, "I say, my wise fellow, do you have a tongue?"

Doodle lowered the flute. "Three of them."

The soldiers guffawed. What a perfect simpleton!

"Three!" said the captain. "How three?"

"One in my mouth and two in my shoes," Doodle answered.

The captain cleared his throat. "Ahem, I see. Very good,

if you're so well supplied with tongues, tell me what sort of a hostelry you operate here," waving a hand at the stable.

"This time of day it's an in, sir."

The captain rolled his eyes at his men, who answered with laughter. "Well, is it an inn, or isn't it? What does the time of day have to do with it?"

"In the afternoon it's an *in,* sir, when all the gentlemen come riding in, and in the morning it's an *out,* when they ride away again."

Now the soldiers weren't sure whether they were laughing at this Yankee bumpkin or at their own leader.

"So it's a barn for horses?" demanded the captain.

"Lord, no, sir," said Doodle. "Horses in this country are way too wild for riding."

"Then what *do* your gentlemen ride?"

"Rabbits, sir."

"Rabbits?"

"Except out West, sir, where the rabbits are too fierce."

"And what do they ride there?"

"Frogs, sir."

"Frogs!"

"Except in the wilderness, where the frogs are untamed."

The captain gritted his teeth. "And what do they ride in the wilderness?"

"Grasshoppers."

They went on like this until the captain was reduced to stammering, and his men had to lead him away.

Soldiers kept arriving from England and the colonists kept fuming against the king. It wasn't long before the two sides faced off and stared at one another down the barrels of muskets. They yelled threats. They yelled insults. By and by the shouts turned to shots and they had a regular war.

The English soldiers wore tall black hats of beaver skin, bright red coats with brass buttons, britches the color of cream, black leggings, and shiny black shoes. When they fought they stood in lines as straight and neat as the teeth of a comb. The rebel colonists dressed any which way, in jerkins and tail coats, in wolfskins and quilts, and they fought like a swarm of bees, swooping and stinging and darting away.

Wherever the shots flew, Doodle rode among the rebels on a swaybacked pony, playing jig tunes on his flute to keep their spirits up. His jacket was stitched together from scraps of cloth in a dozen colors. His britches were fashioned from an old saddle blanket. And as for leggings and shoes, why, he didn't have any. His bare toes wriggled in tune with his music. Around his neck he wore a bright green scarf, and on his head a cap shaped like a giant slipper. The scarf streamed out behind as he rode, and from the crown of his cap fluttered a turkey feather.

At the sight of him the English soldiers laughed so hard they couldn't aim their muskets. "Will you look at this fine Yankee!" they roared. "Isn't he a fop, isn't he the dandiest macaroni you've ever seen?" They decided they must capture this fool and ship him back to London so the king and everyone at home could see how rude these colonists really were.

Back and forth they chased him, from one end of Boston to the other, the soldiers waving their muskets and Doodle waving his flute. Twice they had him cornered, but Doodle slipped away, for he had smeared his pony's legs with bacon grease. Meanwhile, the colonists were busy stealing two of the English cannons and a wagonload of muskets. Finally the soldiers caught Doodle and marched him onto their ship in the harbor. And who should greet him there but the captain whom he'd already tricked!

"So!" yelled the captain. "If it isn't our sly Yankee. Aren't you the dandy, though. Scarf round your throat, is it? Feather in your cap? Well, let's see how sly you feel after a few weeks in the brig!"

They shoved Doodle into a dark hole and slammed the hatch.

"Starve him!" the captain ordered. "Give him nothing but water! I'll teach him to trifle with an officer of the king!"

Now the first thing Doodle did was to take from his pocket the knife he always carried for cleaning horses' hoofs, and with this he chopped a window through the wall of his cell into the next compartment, which happened to be the captain's pantry. There he found cider, cheese, bread, sausage, a candle, and a tinderbox. He lit the candle and sat back to enjoy the captain's food. Next he took his knife and bored through another wall of his cell. Putting his nose to this hole, he smelled gunpowder.

"Water!" he yelled.

In a moment the guard opened the hatch and lowered a jug on a rope. Doodle put the cork in his pocket, poured the water through the hole into the chamber filled with gunpowder, gave a tug on the rope, and yelled, "More water!"

The guard refilled the jug, Doodle emptied it through the

gunpowder hole, tugged the rope, and cried, "Still more water!"

"He's the thirstiest devil in creation!" the guard swore.

After three days of this, Doodle had turned the gunpowder room into a swamp of black mud. That night he decided it was time to escape. He pouched out his cap and stuffed it full of the captain's biscuits until it looked just like an English soldier's hat. He turned his patchwork coat inside out, and, what do you know, the lining was lobster red. The cork from the jug he burned in the candle flame until it was sooty, and this he rubbed on his bare feet and legs to make them look as black as an English soldier's shoes and leggings.

From the next chamber he could hear the captain getting ready for bed. To hurry him along toward sleep, Doodle played a drowsy tune on his flute. Pretty soon the captain was snoring. Doodle crawled through the pantry, helped himself to the captain's medals, which he pinned onto his own chest, then stole out the door, up the stairs, and onto the deck. It was dark, but the medals on his jacket gleamed in the lantern light. Speaking in the captain's gruff voice he ordered two sailors to row him ashore, which they promptly did.

On the wharf he found his pony tied to a flagpole. He climbed on, medals jangling, and in two winks he was clip-clopping away. The sailors scratched their heads to see their captain riding off into the city of rebels on a swaybacked beast in the middle of the night. A moment later a ruckus broke out on the ship, bells ringing, muskets firing, voices hollering, "Escape, escape!" By then, Doodle was long gone.

Well, the captain was fit to be tied. His pantry was bare,

his medals were missing, his gunpowder had been ruined, and somehow his witless prisoner had slipped from under his very nose. He spluttered from the bow of his ship to the stern, yelling at his men to go catch the plug-ugly, addlebrained, snake-tongued Yankee rogue.

The soldiers turned Boston upside down, looking for Doodle, but all they gained by their searching were blisters on the soles of their feet. He led them into blind alleys, into bogs, into packs of sharp-toothed dogs, into one fix after another.

Before long the English colonels heard about this Yankee who was making a fool of their army, and they turned red in the face. Pretty soon the generals caught wind of the scandal, and their beards trembled. By and by the king himself, away over in London, learned of this cheeky rebel, and his jowls quivered. "I want his head on a platter!" he roared. "I want his gizzard toasted on a spit! I want his finger bones for stirring my tea!"

A hundred pairs of eyes would not have been enough to keep track of Doodle. Wherever the English armies fought the rebels, from the mountains of New Hampshire to the swamps of Georgia, from the frozen fields of Pennsylvania to the fishy waters of the Carolinas, there Doodle turned up on his swaybacked pony, wearing a turkey feather in his cap and playing jigs on his flute. It drove the English soldiers mad to see him. Why couldn't they lay their hands on him? He was as slippery as a pickle. Once they trapped him in a barn, shot him full of holes, stuck him with their bayonets; but what they'd killed turned out to be a sack of potatoes dressed up to look like Doodle. Another time they set fire to him, and he burned really well, because what they set afire was only a sack of straw wearing his clothes. Another time they shoved him into the ocean, but the body wouldn't drown, since it was only a log in a patchwork coat.

To make things worse, the rebels were getting the best of the fighting. Having a war with these colonists was like playing chess against a band of monkeys. They didn't know the rules, never lined up where you could have a go at them, dressed in furs and woods-colored clothes so you could hardly see them. It was enough to make a grown man cry, the way they sneaked around, hiding behind trees, jumping out of haystacks, crawling through mud and shooting at you from every direction of the compass.

Things were going so badly for the English that the captains began to bite their nails, the colonels gnashed their teeth, the generals pulled their hair, and the king ranted and raved in his palace, throwing dishes at his servants and kicking stools. None of it did any good. Things went from bad to worse. Finally the king told his generals to come home and leave those beastly colonists alone in their beastly wilderness. The generals told the colonels, the colonels told the captains, the captains told the foot soldiers, and the foot soldiers cheered. At Yorktown they surrendered to General Washington while the ragtag rebels looked on. And just when the English commander was handing over the sword, who should come riding up on his pony and tootling on his flute but the trickiest rebel of them all, that dandy Yankee Doodle. There was a grin on him as wide and bright as the crescent moon.

Greenland Whale Fishery

[TRADITIONAL]

'Twas in eighteen hundred and fifty-three,
On June the thirteen day,
That our gallant ship her anchor weighed,
And for Greenland sailed away, brave boys,
For Greenland sailed away.

The lookout in the cross-trees stood
With a spyglass in his hand,
"There's a whale, there's a whale, there's a whalefish!" he cried,
"She blows out every span, brave boys,
She blows out every span."

The captain stood on the quarter-deck,
And a fine little man was he.
"Overhaul! Overhaul! Let your davit tackles fall,
And launch your boats for the sea, brave boys,
And launch your boats for the sea."

Now the boats were launched and the men aboard,
And the whale was in full view,
Resolved was each seaman bold
To steer where the whalefish blew, brave boys,
To steer where the whalefish blew.

We struck that whale and the line paid out,
But she made a flunder with her tail,
And the boat capsized and four men were drowned,
And we never caught that whale, brave boys,
We never caught that whale.

"To lose the whale," our captain cried,
"It grieves my heart full sore,
But to lose four of my gallant men,
It grieves me ten times more, brave boys,
It grieves me ten times more."

Oh, Greenland is a dreadful place,
A land that's never never green,
Where there's ice and snow and the whalefishes blow,
And daylight's seldom seen, brave boys,
And daylight's seldom seen.

Captain Jeremiah Quick thought like a whale. No matter where the beasts lurked, he sensed their huge breathing, heard their vast heartbeats. Standing on deck in pitch-darkness he could feel them turn in their sleep. By listening to his own belly he could tell when they were feeding. When they swam, he put his nose to the wind and pointed the direction.

"And why shouldn't I know the ways of whales?" he would say. "I'm a sea creature from stem to stern. I have webs between my toes. My blood's nothing more than salt water thickened with a little red bile."

The sailors of his crew believed the captain's blood must be salty enough for codfish and mackerel to swim in. They swore that barnacles grew on the old man's ribs. They imagined eels wriggling through his gray whiskers. His eyes reminded them of the staring dark bullet-hole eyes of a shark. He was a dangerous skipper to work under, for nothing the sea could throw his way ever frightened him, no storm, no whirlpool, no tentacled monster. Besides, he did not know what it meant to be tired. He never rested, never let you loaf, never quit hunting until his barrels were full. Any way you measured it, he was a hard master. But if you wanted to catch the moody, far-wandering whales and leave your pockets heavy with gold after a voyage, there was no better man to sail under than Captain Jeremiah Quick.

From the age of seven onward, sailing was about all he ever did. He started out rowing dinghies in the harbor, became cabin boy on clipper ships, graduated to deckhand, then to mate, and finally to captain of his own whaler. Dry land felt deathly still beneath his seagoing legs. It made him woozy to look at a horizon that did not dip and sway. Fresh food turned his stomach. He could not bear to stay on shore for long, not even on his home island of Nantucket, which was more like a ship than a solid knob of earth. The air on Nantucket was half salt-spray, half fish oil. The sand underfoot shuddered from the hammering of waves. The men living on this watery snout of land went down to plow the sea as men living on the prairies went to plow the fields. The boys of the island built lean-tos with the ribs of sperm whales, the girls played house in the washed-up wrecks of ships, and the women combed their hair with codfish bones.

Captain Quick had always been too busy sailing to pay much mind to the women. His landlady said he ought to get married and raise up little sailors of his own. But he balked at that. He was afraid a wife and children would be like anchor cables, binding him to shore. "I don't need another family," he told her, "I'm already married to my ship, and I've got all my crew for sons."

He truly did think of those sunburned lugs as sons. No matter how gruff he seemed, yelling at them or threatening to heave them overboard, he kept for each of his men a little berth of tenderness in his mind. Every one of his sailors who had drowned or died of a broken neck or fallen sick with a killing disease left in the captain's heart a stinging scar.

His ship went by the name of *Dragon,* which made it sound fierce and swift. But in fact it was a poky old tub, fat in the middle for holding barrels of oil, with three stout masts and only just enough canvas to keep it skidding on course in fair weather. In foul weather, the *Dragon* lurched and bucked along whatever path the storm was taking. "It's no use arguing with a gale," the captain would shout, loving the way winds drove the ship madly on.

He was getting too old for an even wilder ride, the one a harpooned whale gave you after the hook was set in its hump and the line drew taut and the whaleboat sped along jouncing like a cockleshell over the waves. Now and again he still rode in the lead boat and bawled orders to the straining oarsmen, heard the harpooner grunt from the effort of throwing, heard the hemp rope sizzle as it uncoiled from its tub, saw the great flukes rise against the sky and come crashing down, felt the whale sounding and then rising again like a mountain torn free of its roots. Just thinking about that ride made his heart hurry. But nowadays he usually watched the chase, the strike, and the whale's long dragging death through a spyglass from the deck of the *Dragon.*

He often thought the perfect ship would be able to plunge beneath the surface like the whales themselves. He imagined cruising underwater, gazing out through a porthole at the great looming hulks, pushing closer and closer until the skin of his ship rubbed against a huge flank. What beauties he might see, what mysteries he might uncover down there in the depths! Secretly he wanted to become a whale, if only for an hour. Sometimes, daydreaming on deck, he slipped out of his human shape and took on a whale's vast body, full of power and grace, swallowing an acre of fish at a gulp, calling in a thunderous voice to his mates, rising to blow and breathe and turn a huge eye to the sun, beating the sea with his flukes, diving again to glide on the ocean's deep currents. It was a treacherous fancy. If he dwelt in the whale's flesh too long, he would feel the iron point stab into his back, the terrible weight of rope tugging at him, the huge panic filling him, and he would emerge from his daydream with a gasp of fear.

This wonder and fear kept him on the path of the great beasts. He was only truly alive when he was chasing them. Right whale, sperm whale, gray whale, and giant blue, bowhead, humpback, any whale that swam, Captain Quick would hunt it down, and he would chase it through all the seven seas, around Cape Horn and into the South Pacific, past the tangled mountains of Borneo, over the Indian Ocean, around the blunt toe of Africa and away north across the Atlantic to the icy edge of the Arctic. The longer the hunt, the better. No matter how many times he sailed back to port with the ship loaded and every inch of rigging blackened from the melting down of blubber, he never could get enough of whaling. The hunger drove him out again and again onto the ocean. Each time it was harder to quit.

Then late one summer, after a season of hunting in the

waters off Greenland, with every barrel sloshing full of oil and the men staggering from bone-weariness, the *Dragon* was just turning her prow toward Nantucket when the captain ordered a halt. "There's a whale in the neighborhood, my lads," he cried. "I can feel it rising."

The sailors groaned. They were dead on their feet, and thought of nothing but home. Hoping Captain Quick was wrong for once, they scanned the sea between the ship and the icebound shore. There was nothing green on Greenland. It was the dreariest, lonesomest land they had ever seen. Nothing but whalefishes would lure any man into these grim waters.

"Stand by!" yelled the captain. "She's near!"

Sure enough, in a few minutes the lookout high in the crosstree sang, "There she blows!"

Through his telescope the captain glimpsed the blunt snout and tooth-lined jaw of a sperm whale, the most precious of all, and he knew he had to catch it. "We'll go for her!"

"But, Captain," said the first mate, "what'll we do with the oil if we land her?"

The hold was crammed, the deck was crowded with barrels, even the try pots were brimming with oil. The captain knew it was mad to go after another whale; but the hunger seized him and made him shout, "Land her and then I'll worry what to do with her! Go on, lower away, boys, and strike her!"

Climbing into their boats, harpooners in the bow and oarsmen in the middle and steersmen at the rudder, the men grumbled among themselves and gave the captain hard looks.

But they were blue-sea men. Orders were orders. So when their boats hit the water they pulled doggedly toward the spouting whale. From the *Dragon*'s deck the captain watched them row, wishing he were still spry enough to go on that bucking ride with the harpooners.

"It's no blessed use in killing her—" the mate protested.

Captain Quick roared, "When I want your opinion, sir, I'll ask for it!" He was trembling. It frightened him, the way his heart leapt when the whale leapt. She was enormous, a hundred barrels or more. When she breached it was like an island breaking the surface. "Strike her, boys! Strike her!" he bellowed. The wind tore his words loose and scattered them. He clung to the rail, shivering so hard he could barely stay on his feet. "Don't lose her!"

As the lead boat neared the gray bulk a harpooner stood up and cocked his arm.

Throw it true, the captain thought. Strike her deep! "Now, you fool, now!" he cried.

And the harpooner, a speck of a man far beyond earshot, suddenly uncoiled and threw. The shaft plunged into the island of flesh, and a cry ripped from the captain's throat. Before he could shut his mouth the whale heaved its tail in the air, and for an instant the captain felt stifled by a tremendous sorrow, then down boomed the tail, smashing the flimsy boat and driving the six men underwater. The whale dived, tugging harpoon and line and shattered scraps of boat down with it. When at last the surface grew slick again, only two heads showed.

The captain looked away at the frozen, forsaken hump of

Greenland, and kept his gaze there as long as he could bear. But when he looked back at the wreck there were still only two heads bobbing on the sea. Only two, only two, no matter how long he watched and prayed. Four had drowned. Four of his brave boys, gone down to feed his mad hunger. The pain he felt was fiercer than any storm, bleaker than any wind-swept island. It shook him and shamed him and forced him to see how far he had wandered from his true mind, driven so far off course in his hunt for whales. And beyond the slick waters where his men had drowned, the hump of Greenland rose above the sea, mocking him, filling his vision with its gray and frozen back like the greatest whale in the world.

The Ram of Derby

[TRADITIONAL]

As I went down to Derby, all on a market day,
I spied the biggest ram, sir, that ever was fed on hay.

> *And didn't he ramble, ramble,*
> *Rambled all around, in and out of town,*
> *Didn't he ramble, ramble,*
> *Rambled till them butchers cut him down.*

The hair upon this ram's back, sir, it reached up to the sky,
The eagles built their nests there, the young ones dasn't fly.

The horns upon this ram's head, sir, they grew up to the moon,
A boy clumb up in January and didn't get back till June.

This ram he had a tail, sir, it reached way down in Hell,
And every time he waggled that tail, it rung that hotel bell.

The hair on this ram's belly, sir, it reached down to the ground,
The Devil stole a strand of that hair and made his wife a gown.

He rambled on the waterside, he rambled on the land,
But when he went to the butcher's pen, 'twas there he met a man.

The man that butchered this ram, sir, was scairt of his life,
He sent to Philadelphy to get him a four-foot knife.

The man that butchered this ram, sir, was drowned in the blood,
And the boy that held the basin was washed away in the flood.

Took all the boys in our town to roll away his bones,
Took all the girls in our town to roll away the stones.

The man that owned this ram, sir, he was awful rich,
And the man who told this story was a lying son-of-a-gun.

One summer day there was a gaggle of kids lolling on a straw pile in the hog barn at the New Haven County Fair, bragging about the animals their families had raised. Old Granny Barden stood nearby, sucking on her pipe and listening to the young ones gab.

"My sister raised a boar," said a girl, "that was so broad you could set a kitchen table on his back and still have room for the chairs."

"That's nothing," said a boy. "My aunt's got an old sow you can square dance on top of, she's so fat."

"Your aunt's so fat?" said one of the toddlers.

"No, you numbskull—the *sow*."

"You talk about big!" another boy put in. "Why, we got a bull that's bigger than a wagon. When our bull gives a snort and paws the ground, the trees in the pasture shake loose of their roots."

One of the girls said, "But can your bull tug a barn right off its foundation? My uncle's draft mule can do it without working up a lather."

Granny Barden smiled at their talk. Her brown skirt hung flapping over her shoe tops, and she used it like a fence, stepping here and there around the bunch of kids to keep the babies from crawling down off the straw and maybe getting squashed by a hog. The parents were off sashaying through the fair, knowing Granny would look after their little ones.

Another girl piped up. "My momma's hen lays eggs the size of pumpkins. It takes me and my sister both to carry one in from the chicken coop. Momma uses a hammer and chisel to break the shell."

"We've got a fish in our pond," said a boy, "that one day when the cattle was down there drinking ate a calf and spit out the bones on the shore. My daddy killed it by chopping down a tree flat bang on its head, and my momma roasted it all week over a fire, and it fed the whole of our church on Sunday."

Granny Barden drew the pipe from her mouth. She never smoked it, but only chewed on it to keep her tongue from getting lonely when she wasn't talking. "All those animals sound pretty grand," she said, "but they'd look like mice and moles beside a critter I could tell you about."

At the sound of her voice the kids hushed, for they'd sooner hear Granny Barden talk about the long-ago days than eat pie. Even the babies quit trying to crawl down off the straw pile. They sat up on their roly-poly bottoms and tuned their ears.

"All your talk puts me in mind of one time when I was just a little bit of a child about as high as a stump, no bigger than most of you," said Granny, pointing the stem of her pipe at the children, "and how my Uncle Albert raised the most wonderful ram that ever walked the earth."

"We got a ram at our place," said one of the toddlers, "and he's mean and butts like anything."

"Shush up! Shush up and let her talk!" the others hissed.

Granny eased herself down onto the straw and smoothed

the skirt over her creaky old legs. The three babies crawled into her lap. A drifty, faraway look came over her eyes. "The time I'm telling you about was a long while back," she said, "before the world had shrunk down so. The sun was fatter. Moon was fatter. Anything you want to name, there was more of it in those days. More stars, more rainstorms, more black-berries. The grass in the pastures grew way up over your head. An ear of corn was as long as your arm."

The children looked down at their arms, then back at Granny.

"Well, in those days my Uncle Albert was raising sheep, away north up Beaver Creek on the edge of Peat Swamp. Every spring he'd bring his fleece to the market in Derby, and maybe a few old worn-out rams to sell for mutton. He'd sit around with the other farmers and listen to them crow about the prize sheep they'd left back home. Rams too big to fit through barn doors. Ewes that dropped five lambs every spring. Such tales! You know how proud and boastful grown-ups can get when they're trading stories."

The children nodded wisely. They knew, they sure did.

"There was one farmer in particular, he got himself worked into a tizzy, bragging about his sheep. He claimed there wasn't any sheep in the world since Noah came down off the ark that could outdo his prize ram for growing fleece or putting on meat. Well, first one man and then another one said it wasn't so, said they had rams every bit as fine or finer. Before you knew it, they were laying bets."

"Bets! Bets!" the children echoed the word in scandalized whispers. They knew this was a wickedness that grown-ups sometimes practiced.

"Yes," said Granny, "I'm afraid it's true. What they bet was, whichever farmer brought the biggest, fleeciest, meatiest ram to market in Derby the next spring, why, everybody else would mow his hay for him that year. All of them who wanted in on it shook hands together."

"Did your Uncle Albert bet?" said one of the children.

"I'm bound to say he did. He didn't boast, though, and he didn't brag, for that wasn't his way. But he shook hands along with the rest of them. You see, Uncle Albert had a ram he thought would put all the others in the shade."

"It must have been a whopper!" one child yelled.

The others hissed for quiet, and Granny resumed her tale: "By and by the market was over. Uncle Albert went home to his farm on Beaver Creek. That very day he took his biggest ram to the back pasture, right up next to the Peat Swamp, and started in feeding him sweet grasses by the armload. Now that ram went to putting on weight and puffing out with fleece, but not fast enough to satisfy my Uncle Albert. What would make the ram grow faster? he wondered. Well, he thought, what grows fast? Babies, willow trees, and mushrooms. He couldn't see his way clear to feeding the ram with babies— there weren't enough of them on hand, for one thing—so Uncle Albert gathered wagonloads of willow shoots and barrels of mushrooms, and fed up that great big sheep until it couldn't hold any more."

"Did it bust?" said a boy.

"No, it didn't, but it swelled up and swelled up until Uncle Albert had to knock down a stone fence between two pastures just to give him room to spread out. As soon as the ram swallowed those mushrooms and willow shoots, Uncle Albert fed him brambles and grapevines to thicken up his fleece. It seemed like, the more that critter ate, the hungrier he got. And thirsty! Every time the ram drank from Beaver Creek the water level fell two feet. It got to where the water wheels on the mills downstream wouldn't turn for an hour after he'd drunk his fill. Well, Uncle Albert figured he'd better find water somewhere else pretty soon, before every miller in the county came upstream looking for where the trouble was. So he dug a hole in Peat Swamp—you know how boggy that land is—and it wasn't long before the hole filled up with the blackest water you ever saw."

"Black as sin!"

"Black as the Devil's toenails!"

"Black as midnight inside an alligator!"

"That black, and blacker still," said Granny, "and all on account of the peat that gets soaked up in the water. You and me, now, we wouldn't drink such water if it was the last drink on earth. But Uncle Albert's old ram wasn't choosy. He shoved his snout in that hole and slurped that peaty water until the bog started to heave and quake. Lucky thing it was a rainy year, because every time he was just about to drink the bog dry, a storm would come along and fill it up again. Now your peat is a remarkable stuff. Who can tell me what it is?"

The children wriggled on the straw pile, shouting their answers:

"It's rotten old muck!"

"It's mud from before the Flood!"

"It's gunk cleaned out from behind the Devil's ears!"

"I'll tell you what it is," said Granny, her voice getting

very small and the children's eyes growing large. "It's the conglomerated essence of vegetables. It's the alluvium pluvium of grass and bushes and weeds. In short, it's the purest animal food ever invented. A teaspoon of peat has about as much growing power as a whole field of alfalfa. Not many people know that. It's one of history's great secrets. But my Uncle Albert tumbled onto it pretty soon after his ram started drinking from that bog, because inside of thirty minutes his ram was growing so fast you could hear the skin stretch. It grew so high, you could stand west of it in the morning and the sun wouldn't shine over its back until two hours after dawn. It grew so high, a momma eagle built her nest in the curly fleece up between the horns, and when the babies peeped out they were too scared to fly. When the ram wagged its tail the wind started blowing and rang the dinner bell at my house. I don't know how many times I came in early to eat on account of that ram's tail."

"I'm hungry," cried a toddler.

"Me, too!"

"Me, too!"

"Wait, now," said Granny, "and listen to what happened when spring rolled around and it came time for Uncle Albert to take his ram to market. Well, he didn't dare let the critter just walk to Derby, for the stamping of its feet on the ground would have shaken down the chimneys and loosened the chinking on every cabin it passed along the road. There wasn't a wagon in creation big enough to hold it. But Uncle Albert figured a fleet of boats might just about do the trick. So when Beaver Creek flooded that spring, he loaded his ram onto four barges, one for each foot. He tied the barges together and set a fire of wet leaves at the front and back, so the smoke would hide what he was carrying to Derby."

"Keep it a secret!" cried a girl.

"That's right, honey. He didn't want to give those other farmers a chance to back out on their deal. Well, Uncle Albert and his ram floated downstream and plowed that creek as straight as a furrow. In a little while they tied up at the wharf in Derby, down by the market square, and all you could see was a great big cloud of smoke. Out stepped Uncle Albert. The other farmers were already standing around, waiting for him. What'd you bring to show, Albert, a burning haystack? they said. Naw, he said, just a bitty old thin-fleeced ram that gets cold without a fire. The farmers had their sheep hidden under blankets and inside wagons. They all shook hands again on their bet, saying whichever man showed the finest, fleshiest, fleeciest ram, well then, everybody else would mow his hay for him."

"Wait till they see what Uncle Albert's brought!" one of the kids shouted. All the children squirmed on the straw, impatient to get Uncle Albert's glorious ram unloaded from the barges.

"They didn't have long to wait, sweetlings, because pretty soon the other men had their rams on show, and a handsomer flock of sheep you never saw. Any one of them would have taken best of fair here in New Haven. But then it came Uncle Albert's turn. He poured water on the fires in his barges, and while the smoke drifted away he led his ram up onto the bricks of the market square. Why, it shook the glass in the windows. It threw the whole of Derby into the shade. Lord, you should have seen folks scuttle out of the way! They thought it was an avalanche, a blizzard, a mountain of snow on four legs. They didn't know *what* it was, until they bent their heads way back and looked up to the sky and saw that muzzle chewing on grapevines and saw those curly horns scraping the clouds. Great day in the morning! they shouted. It wasn't a four-legged mountain at all, but a ram! Well, those other sheep farmers opened their mouths and left them open. They couldn't say a word, just threw blankets over their own prize rams or hid them away in wagons."

The children clapped their hands. "Uncle Albert won!"

"He won, all right. The men took whetstones and sharpened their scythes, knowing they would need them to cut Uncle Albert's meadow. The scythes came in handy right then and there for shearing the fleece from that ram. The farmers climbed on ladders up to the neck and worked their way toward the tail, mowing as they went. You couldn't see a thing but their hats bobbing up over the top of the fleece. The wool filled the marketplace and spread into the nearby streets. There was enough wool from that ram to keep a hundred weavers busy all year and to make enough coats for every soul in Connecticut. They sheared for three days. And then it came time for butchering."

The children squealed with horror. "They ain't going to butcher *our* ram, are they?"

"They had to, honey. Uncle Albert couldn't keep on feeding a mountain, could he? The peat bog was about wrung dry. The creek didn't hold enough to water him with. So Uncle Albert had to lay that old ram low. But he couldn't bear to do it himself. Nobody in Derby had the nerve to do it, and nobody in New Haven. Finally they had to send to Philadelphia for a butcher, who said there wasn't any four-legged beast he couldn't handle. He showed up toting a knife that was the size of a wagon tongue. Everybody stood way back. And that man from Philadelphia, he waltzed to and fro a few dozen times, gathering his courage, before he started in butchering. Well, he lived to regret it for about half a minute, because the blood from that ram drowned the butcher and turned Beaver Creek as red as sunset, and the creek flowed red into the Housatonic River, and people say the Housatonic turned the Atlantic Ocean red halfway to England. I don't know for sure about that, because I never sailed out there to see for myself, but I can believe it. What I do know is that after a while everybody pitched in to help with the butchering, and it took them seven days and seven nights, and when they were finished the children piled up bones higher than the church steeple, and nobody in New Haven County ate a single thing for six months besides Uncle Albert's mutton."

Granny stuck the pipe back in her mouth. The babies tilted their goggle eyes up at her. The toddlers made faces like fishes. The older kids scratched their heads or tugged on their ears. Finally, one of them said, "Is every bit of that true, Granny?"

"Of course it is," said Granny. "You take that fleece, for instance. It was so long and thick you could lace both your shoes with a single strand of it. See here?" And to prove the truth of it she pulled up her lanky skirts to reveal her high-topped shoes, each one snugly laced and tied in a neat white bow.

Frog Went A-Courting

[TRADITIONAL]

Froggie went a-courting and he did ride, uh-hum!
Froggie went a-courting and he did ride,
Sword and pistol by his side, uh-hum, uh-hum, uh-hum!

He rode till he came to Miss Mousie's den, uh-hum!
Rode till he came to Mousie's den,
Said, "Miss Mousie are you within?" uh-hum, uh-hum, uh-hum!

He put Miss Mousie on his knee, uh-hum!
Put Miss Mousie on his knee,
Said, "Miss Mousie, will you marry me?" uh-hum, uh-hum, uh-hum!

"Not without my Uncle Rat's consent," uh-unh!
"Without my Uncle Rat's consent,
I wouldn't marry the President!" uh-unh, uh-unh, uh-unh!

Now Uncle Rat came a-riding home, uh-hum!
Uncle Rat came a-riding home,
Said, "Who's been here while I been gone?" uh-hum, uh-hum, uh-hum!

Uncle Rat laughed till he shook his sides, uh-hum!
Uncle Rat laughed till he shook his sides,
To think his niece could be a bride, uh-hum, uh-hum, uh-hum!

"Where will the wedding supper be?" uh-hum!
"Where will the wedding supper be?"
"Yonder under the hickory tree," uh-hum, uh-hum, uh-hum!

"What will the wedding supper be?" uh-hum!
"What will the wedding supper be?"
"Two blue beans and a black-eyed pea," uh-hum, uh-hum, uh-hum!

First to arrive was a little black bug, uh-hum!
First to arrive was a little black bug,
Fell into the whiskey jug, uh-hum, uh-hum, uh-hum!

Next to arrive was a garter snake, uh-hum!
Next to arrive was a garter snake,
Wrapped itself round the wedding cake, uh-hum, uh-hum, uh-hum!

Last to arrive was a big tomcat, uh-hum!
Last to arrive was a big tomcat,
Ate Miss Mousie and Uncle Rat, uh-hum, uh-hum, uh-hum!

Froggie jumped into the lake, uh-hum!
Froggie jumped into the lake,
And there he was et by a water snake, uh-hum, uh-hum, uh-hum!

Now that was the end of him and her, uh-hum!
That was the end of him and her,
Guess there won't be no tadpoles covered with fur, uh-hum, uh-hum, uh-hum!

*O*ne day Frog decided he had lived by himself long enough. It was time to get married. But who on earth would love a fellow as ugly as he was? He studied himself in the mirror: shiny green skin covered with spots, bulgy eyes, wrinkled nose, a mouth like a coal bucket, a curling red worm of a tongue, great gangly legs and floppy feet, no tail at all. His voice, he thought, was even worse than his looks. When he talked it sounded like rocks clattering in the bottom of a bucket. When he sang it was like thunder caught in a cave.

"There are plenty of sweet frogs who'd gladly jump at you," his mother used to tell him.

"They might jump," Frog would answer, "but I wouldn't be in the neighborhood when they landed."

He didn't want to marry anybody with green skin and bulgy eyes. He would much prefer a sweetheart who looked nothing like a frog. Tiny eyes would be nice, and fur, and a real snout for a nose, and maybe even a tail. Thinking that, his memory began to itch. It reminded him of somebody. Now who?

Sighing, he got dressed up to go courting, hoping he would know the right bride when he saw her. He put on his red vest, his blue britches with the bright blue stitches, and a wide-brimmed hat with a tuft of milkweed fluff in the band. Then he stood back to have a gander at himself in the mirror. Ah, he thought, what's the use! Even in that get-up, he still looked as ugly as a stump covered with fungus. Maybe a little touch of the soldier would help. From over the mantel he took down his sword, strapped it around his waist, and stuck his pistol in the belt. He frowned. There was no way to hide it. Sword and pistol or not, the fellow who blinked out at him from the mirror was still a frog and nothing but a frog.

But since he was all dandied up, he figured he might as well go out anyway and try his luck. Off he went, hopping down the road, the sword rattling every time he landed. He hadn't gone but a little piece when he came by Miss Mouse's den, and there was Miss Mouse herself, sitting on the stoop in the sunshine gnawing on a pine cone. Well, Frog had seen Miss Mouse quite a few times before, and never thought much about her one way or the other. But today, seeing her in the sunlight with her tiny paws on the pine cone and her tail curled up and her little squinchy brown eyes blinking, it was like a kick in the belly. He stopped in the middle of the road and couldn't budge.

Miss Mouse spat out the husk of a pine nut. "Why, hello, Mr. Frog. You're looking mighty fancy."

Frog just squatted there.

"Where are you off to, dressed so fine?" said Miss Mouse.

Frog's mouth sagged open.

"Looks to me," she said, "like you're going courting."

Frog's long red tongue dangled out, but he couldn't bring himself to say a word.

"Don't tell me you came here courting me!" Miss Mouse cried.

Without even thinking, Frog jerked his head up and down.

Miss Mouse began to pat herself with her paws. "And here I am in my oldest overalls and a straw hat with holes in it and my fur uncombed!"

Just then a fly buzzed by. Frog snapped it up, and that loosened his tongue for talking. In a rush he blurted out, "Miss Mouse, I'd love you even if you were wrapped in old snakeskin and porcupine bristles, you're so beautiful, you make my heart dizzy, I can't live another day without you, O gracious me, I'll make you the warmest nest and stuff it with goose down and haul in wagonloads of seeds and do everything up grand if you'll only marry me. What do you say?"

"Well . . ." Miss Mouse took her tail and swung the end of it in a circle, considering. "Do you promise to hop when I say hop?"

"I promise."

"And do you promise not to wear that ridiculous sword and pistol in the house?"

"I do, I do."

"Will you keep your lovely green skin all polished up so it shines?"

Frog looked down in puzzlement at his belly, which swelled in a green curve between his red vest and his blue britches. "If it pleases you, my dear."

"And will you sing for me any time I ask?"

"*Sing?* With my rattly bucket of a voice?"

"Don't you say such a thing! I've listened to you go by here many a time, singing for all you're worth, and a mellower, moodier, goose-bumpier voice I never heard."

Frog smiled. Then he started humming. Then he puffed up his cheeks and sang:

> Keemo kimo, where O where?
> Who stole Skunk's long underwear?
> He looked high and he looked low,
> But what thief stole it he never did know.

"Lovely," Miss Mouse sighed, "just lovely."

He wanted to go get married right then and there, but she said, Dear me, no, she couldn't do a thing without asking Uncle Rat, and who knew when he'd roll back in from town? She wouldn't even marry the President without Uncle Rat's say-so. So Frog sat there beside Miss Mouse in the sunshine, picking the nuts out of pine cones and drumming his toes on the stoop, waiting.

By and by, here came Uncle Rat, red-eyed and wobbly in the knees. He had a slew of friends between here and town, and always stopped to see every last one of them. Since he never could turn down the offer of a bite to eat or a drop to drink, he was fat enough to pass for a bare-tailed raccoon.

"Uncle, dear," said Miss Mouse, "I'd like you to meet—"

"Meat?" Uncle Rat slapped his belly. "If you insist, my dear. I suppose I could do with a slice or two. And would you have any applesauce to go with it?"

Miss Mouse pursed her lips. "Not food, uncle. I'd like you to meet a visitor. Here's Mr. Frog come a-courting."

"Fog?" said Uncle Rat, squinting his red eyes. "Why, yes, isn't it terrible? Worst I've seen."

"Not fog, uncle. *Frog.*"

Uncle Rat sniffed. His eyes weren't doing him much good, but his nose still worked. "I smell a stranger, niece. Has somebody come here snooping while I've been gone?"

Miss Mouse pushed Frog up under Uncle Rat's nose.

"Well, lookit here," said Uncle Rat, "if it isn't Mr. Frog dressed up like a Christmas tree." Uncle Rat's eyes narrowed into fiery slits. "And just what are you after?"

"I was hopping down the road," said Frog, "and there was Miss Mouse with her tail curled up, and the sun shining, and the birds swishing by overhead, and—"

"He's come asking for my paw," Miss Mouse put in.

"But your pa's dead and gone, honey," said Uncle Rat.

"Not my daddy. My *paw*. He wants to *marry* me."

"Tie the knot," said Frog.

"Have a wedding," said Miss Mouse.

"Get hitched," said Frog.

It took Uncle Rat a while to figure out what Miss Mouse and Frog were saying, but when at last he understood, he squinted from one to the other, then he started laughing, and he laughed until his belly bounced. "You two get married! What are you going to raise, furry tadpoles?"

"Now, uncle, don't make rude jokes. Just say yes."

"But who'll sew your wedding gown?" said Uncle Rat.

"Great-grandma Rat from Pumpkin Town," replied Miss Mouse, for she had already figured everything out.

"But who'll make music for the dance?"

"A dozen crickets in fancy pants."

"But where will the wedding supper be?"

"Yonder under the hickory tree."

"And what will the wedding supper be?"

"Two blue beans and a black-eyed pea."

Uncle Rat stroked his whiskers. "I tell you what. Throw in a bushel more to eat and a jug or so to drink, and I'll give my blessing."

Miss Mouse hugged Frog, and he swung her around until her feet lifted clear off the ground. No more being lonesome! He made up a song to celebrate:

> There once was a Frog
> And a pretty little Mouse
> Moved into a log
> And set up house.
> She was the mammy
> And he was the pappy.
> They started a family
> And felt mighty happy.

Frog and Miss Mouse invited everybody they could think of to the wedding—everybody, that is, except ornery Mr. Cat. With his mean temper, any party he came to he was sure to spoil.

By and by the day rolled around, and the guests started coming. First to arrive was Doodle Bug, who fell into the whiskey jug. Next one there was Garter Snake, who wrapped himself around the wedding cake. Third in line was Bumble Bee, playing the fiddle across her knee. Fourth was Mole with a great big grin, playing on the mandolin. Fifth was Skunk, tapping his toes, playing on his aunt's banjo. Cow strolled up, and Plow Horse, too, and Goat and Hog in brand new shoes. Then came a dozen crickets in fancy pants and a hundred fleas and a thousand ants.

Well, before you knew it, Frog and Miss Mouse were husband and wife. You should have seen the two of them kissing, right there in broad daylight! Bee sawed on her fiddle, mole played mandolin, and Skunk made that banjo ring. The crickets sang, and the fleas did a few turns in the air. The ants built themselves up into a pyramid, one atop another, and when they got tired they tumbled down in a heap. Uncle Rat poured Doodle Bug out of the jug, then drank off the whiskey to keep it from spoiling. Folks ate and laughed until they began to stretch at the seams. Everybody had a high old time.

Then a little wind blew up, with the smell of danger on it, and a chill came over the wedding party. Before you knew it, here crept Cat, his nose twitching, his teeth showing.

"Why didn't anybody invite me?" he growled.

"We f-f-forgot," said Frog.

"We didn't forget," said Miss Mouse, all white and crinkly in her wedding gown.

"Oh, yes, we did," Frog insisted.

"Oh, no, we didn't! Mr. Cat, you are the last creature we wanted to have at our wedding."

"Well, here I am, last of all," Cat snarled, "just in time to finish you off," and with that he leapt on Miss Mouse and gobbled her up.

Uncle Rat waddled over to Cat, shaking his paw and huffing. "Here, now, you can't go eating my niece." He swatted Cat on the nose. "Let me see her right now!"

"You want to see her? Then go see her." Cat opened his jaws as wide as they would go and swallowed Uncle Rat.

The wedding guests ran for dear life, even Horse and Cow and Hog and Goat, who didn't want Cat nipping at their heels. Only Skunk stayed behind, to eat the scraps. Cat wouldn't mess with Skunk. Poor Frog stood there a minute with one hand on his sword and the other on his pistol, trying to get up his courage.

"What are you gawking at, greenskin?" said Cat, licking his lips.

Frog thumped his foot on the ground. "Give me back my wife!"

"You're welcome to go see her, too." Cat yawned.

The sight of that pink throat and those glistening fangs scared Frog out of his wits. His heart said, Stay and fight. But feet said, Run. Feet won the argument. His hind legs jerked and he took off hopping, couldn't help himself, hopped and hopped until he landed with a splat in the lake. Down he sank, miserable, not even bothering to swim, not paying any mind, down and down—until he drifted past Water Snake, who swallowed him in one gulp.

Well, some folks say that was the end of him and her, and there never would be any tadpoles covered with fur. But that just goes to show how little some folks know. Because, you see, even if Uncle Rat had been wanting to get swallowed, the last creature on earth he would have asked to do the swallowing was that filthy old Cat. And Miss Mouse wasn't about to stay cooped up anywhere unless Frog was there, too. So down inside Cat's belly they started biting and kicking and scratching. Cat gritted his teeth and held on. Then Miss Mouse took the crinkly lace hem of her wedding gown and tickled him in the gizzard. And that was more than Cat could stand. He choked and sneezed and shook all over, and finally coughed them up.

Away they ran, quick as blazes, straight to their den. "Where's my lovely Frog?" Miss Mouse asked Skunk, who was still finishing the crumbs from the party.

"Water Snake ate him," said Skunk.

Miss Mouse wailed. She crawled down into the den, where she cried and cried. Nothing Uncle Rat could say would comfort her.

Now all this while, down inside Water Snake, Frog was thinking he might as well die, with his wife all gobbled up. But then he got to thinking how Miss Mouse loved to hear him sing, and how maybe he ought to go sit on her stoop and sing a song to remember her by. Well, he got all ferocious and excited, wanting to sing for Miss Mouse. So he took his sword and chopped a hole between Water Snake's ribs, and out he swam. He hit the shore already hopping, hopped straight to Miss Mouse's den, sat back on his haunches and sang:

> Frog loved Mousie with all his heart.
> He hoped that they would never part.
> But Cat came along and gobbled her down,
> And now Frog thinks he might as well drown.

Deep inside the den, Miss Mouse heard him singing. Was it Frog, or the angel of Frog? She made the dust fly, running out to see. One hug around that fat green neck, one kiss on those slick green lips, and she knew it wasn't any angel, but dear old Frog himself. And Frog, he swelled up with joy and sang harder.

On Top of Old Smoky

[TRADITIONAL]

On top of Old Smoky,
All covered with snow,
I lost my true lover,
From courting too slow.

Now courting's a pleasure
And parting's a grief,
For a falsehearted lover
Is worse than a thief.

They'll tell you they love you
To give your heart ease,
And as soon as your back's turned,
They'll love who they please.

I wrote him a letter,
In red rosy lines,
He sent it back to me
All twisted in twine.

He says, "Keep your love letters
And I'll keep mine.
You write to your true love,
And I'll write to mine.

"Your parents is against me
And mine is the same.
If I'm down in your book, love,
Please blot out my name.

"Now I can love little
And I can love long.
I can love an old sweetheart
Till a new one comes along.

"I can hug them and kiss them
And prove to them kind.
I can turn my back on them
And alter my mind.

"My horses ain't hungry,
They won't eat your hay,
So fare thee well, darling,
I'm going away.

"I'll drive on to Georgia,
And write you my mind.
My mind is to marry,
And leave you behind."

I'll go on Old Smoky
On the mountain so high,
Where the wild birds and turtledoves
Can hear my sad cry.

As sure as the dewdrops
Fall on the green corn,
Last night I was with him,
Tonight he is gone.

*H*anna lived with her old parents away up a mountain in Tennessee, and the worst of it was, not a single boy worth marrying lived within a two-day walk of her cabin. This mountain was so far lost and gone that some days the people who farmed up there didn't even have weather. They'd roll out of bed, peer between the curtains, not see anything at all, neither rain nor sunshine, neither clouds nor clear sky, and they'd get so downhearted they'd go back to sleep.

Other times they'd get too much weather. In winter, storms would blunder into the mountain and circle around looking for a way out, all the while burying that peak under feet and feet of snow. Or a fog would drift by and get snagged and stick around for days, fog so thick it swallowed words, and folks could hardly hear themselves talk. If you came riding up the valley in a time of fog you wouldn't even see the peak, you'd only see the ghost of a mountain shimmering against the sky like a shadow on water—like a mountain made of smoke—and that's why people there called it Old Smoky.

It wasn't much of a place for farming—stony and steep— which was the reason all of Hanna's brothers took off as soon as their beards came in, and all her sisters rode away as soon as they found men to marry. Hanna was the last child born and the last one at home to look after her parents, who were old enough to be her grandmother and grandfather. In spring she planted tobacco, in summer she hoed it, in fall she gathered it leaf by leaf and hung it in the barn to dry. All year round she tended the cow and hogs, hunted chicken eggs, carried wood for the stove. Every night she had to rub her mother's feet, they were so knotted up with rheumatism, and had to read five pages out of the Bible to her father, whose eyes were glazed over with a film like a skim of ice.

Hanna loved them well enough. But when her mother grew too crippled up to cook or wash, and her father grew too dim-sighted to hitch the horses or plow, and she had every last living thing to do all by herself, then where would she be? And when they took sick, and when by and by they died, what sort of life would that be, alone by herself on a lost-and-gone mountain raising burley tobacco?

Most weeks, the only time she met a soul besides her parents was in church on Sunday and Wednesday. Every man there was already hitched to somebody else, except for the gangly boys, who were still praying for whiskers, and the old geezers, half of them widowers and the other half dyed-in-the-wool bachelors, all of them with quavery voices and mouths like groundhog holes.

One time a blacksmith came visiting on the mountain to see about setting himself up a shop. His face wasn't the sort you'd want to put in a picture, but he was about the right age, he wore a clean shirt, and he didn't look away when he caught Hanna giving him the eye. Before too many Sundays had gone by, she was hanging on his arm all the way home from church. He didn't talk much. In fact, he scarcely talked at all. But Hanna could tell from his eyes that he had entire speeches and sermons on love locked up in his heart, just waiting on his stubborn tongue to set them loose.

So they walked home from church, Sunday noon and Wednesday evening, week after week, Hanna chatting and the blacksmith staring at his boots. As soon as they reached the front door of her cabin, he would lift his hat, give her a bow, then rush off like a colt let out to pasture.

Things weren't getting very far very fast. So one day Hanna asked him, "When are you going to come sit up with me?"

"By and by," the blacksmith answered, which for him was quite a string of words.

"How about this Saturday?" she said.

He nodded yes to that, dashed away, and came back Saturday evening with a fiddle under his arm. He sat down next to her and held on tight to the fiddle, as if he were dangling over a cliff and that fiddle were the last bush he could hold on by. Hanna's father shelled walnuts at the table and her mother sewed patches for a quilt beside the fire. Hanna asked the smithy about horses and iron and the best wood for burning in a forge, but he didn't answer more than a word or two. She figured he never would talk with her parents sitting there, so she rubbed her mother's feet and read some Bible to her father.

"It sure is getting late," she observed.

"Now there's a funny thing," said her mother, "but I'm not the least little bit sleepy."

"Me neither," said her father.

"I believe I could sit here patching for hours and hours," said her mother.

"I do love the smell of these walnuts," said her father.

Hanna gave a big sigh, knowing they would fall asleep before too long right where they sat. She made another try at the blacksmith. Was it true, she asked him, that shoes for oxen came in two pieces on account of their cloven hoofs? Would those ox shoes fit the cloven-footed Devil, did he think? Which took more skill to make, candleholders or door-latches? Did water in a cedar barrel temper iron harder than water in a barrel of oak? He'd say yes or no, shrug his shoulders, lift his eyebrows, scrape the bristles on his chin. Keeping a conversation going with him was like keeping a fire lit in a rainstorm. But Hanna didn't give up. She kept throwing on the kindling, question after question. Along about midnight her father slumped down on the table, her mother sagged onto the hearth, and the two old folks started wheezing and snoring, dead to the world.

"Now you can say whatever's in your heart," Hanna told the blacksmith. "They wouldn't wake up if you fired off a musket."

Instead of shooting a gun, he did something even harder on the nerves, which was to play his fiddle. The caterwauling sounds he dragged out of that instrument gave pain to every dog within five miles. Hanna herself, only three feet away, wondered if noise could stop a person's heart. Misreading the tears that came to her eyes, the blacksmith played all the harder.

After what seemed to Hanna like several hours of unbroken scrawking and screeching, he ran out of tunes and quit. In the first moment of silence she had an inkling of how it might feel to be cradled in the comforting arms of God. She swallowed, testing her ears. She dabbed her eyes with the corner of her apron. It was a measure of how set she was on marriage that she did not kick the blacksmith out of the cabin right then and there. Instead she declared, "That sure was remarkable. I never heard anybody play like that before."

He drew himself up straight in the chair and glowed with pleasure.

If he doesn't talk to me about love pretty soon now, after what I've sat through, Hanna decided, I'll wring his thick neck for him.

Time and again he seemed about ready to declare himself, the way his face twitched and trembled, like a pot of custard working up to a boil. But each time, instead of talking, he scraped on the fiddle.

By the first rooster crow, the blacksmith's shirt was soaked through from the labor of his fiddling, and Hanna's heart was as cold as day-old ashes. In the early light he gazed at her with a question stamped on his homely face. Making a great effort he brought himself to say, "Will you?"

"No," Hanna replied, and being a tender soul she added, "No, I don't believe I will, thank you kindly all the same."

The next look that came over the blacksmith's face was one of tremendous relief. He stood up, gave an awkward bow, tucked the fiddle under his arm, and fled on down the mountain, never to be seen in those parts again.

The seasons rolled their great wheel across Old Smoky, three more winters of smothering snow, three more blistering summers. Hanna's mother got to where she couldn't even hobble about the cabin on her own two feet, the rheumatism was so bad. Hanna's father stayed indoors to keep the old woman company and to carry her about when she needed moving. His eyes were so frosted over with cataracts that he wasn't much use outdoors, anyhow, couldn't see to plow a furrow, couldn't see to split wood. Every chore that needed doing, Hanna had to do it. She began to feel like a meadow of sweet flowers which had budded up, bloomed, and would soon go to seed.

Then early one summer in a time of fog, she was down on her knees in the dirt setting out tobacco seedlings when she heard on the mountain road the rattle of a wagon and a man's deep voice gaily singing. Lord, Lord, she thought, who on earth might that be? She squinted down the road and saw a dark splotch in the fog, like a stain on a pillowcase. Presently it took on the humpy shape of a canvas-topped wagon, bumping along over the stony track with a man swaying on the seat. Even in the fog she could tell from his gay voice and his thicket of curly dark hair that he was a stranger, no one she'd ever seen before on Old Smoky.

The wagon drew to a stop beside her, the man smiled down, and said, "Might you be the lady of this here farm?"

Still kneeling there in the dirt, a tobacco plant in her mud-caked hand, Hanna answered, "Yes," and then, remembering her mother, she added in a fluster, "No."

The man laughed, and the sound made her think of rain on the shake roof. "If there's one thing I like," he said, "it's a woman who knows her own mind."

Hanna was thankful for the smudges of dirt on her cheeks, which hid the blushes. No one had ever called her a woman before. Always it had been girl, girl, girl. "My mother's in the cabin," she said.

"Well, then, in the cabin is where I'd like to be. Could you let up in your work long enough to take me? I've got a wagon full of notions to show you and your mother."

So, thought Hanna, he's a peddler, the worst sort of man

for sweetening up to girls and then leaving them behind. "I've got to get this tobacco in the ground," she said.

"Then I'll help you. Double hands make light work."

Without so much as a by-your-leave, the peddler climbed down from his wagon, turned up his sleeves, and started in to plant. As he and Hanna worked, reaching into the box for seedlings, now and again their fingers brushed. All the while he kept up a bright trickle of talk—about the country he had traveled through on his peddler's rounds, from Virginia over to Arkansas, from Mississippi on down to Florida, about the characters he'd met, about the sights there were to see in this glorious world. For Hanna, who'd never seen much except the top of Old Smoky, this talk was a dizzy delight. Her opinion of peddlers grew more favorable every minute.

Presently the fog burned away and the sun shone through, and she got a good look at this stranger. What she saw made her chew her lip, for he had a face you could wear a picture of in your locket, a face you could stare at for an hour and not get tired.

When they finished with the tobacco, Hanna put the planting boxes on her shoulder and started back toward the cabin.

The peddler grabbed her by the elbow. "Hold on, now. No use in you walking while I've got my wagon here. Those feet are too dainty for this rough ground."

Hanna knew her feet were sturdy, but she didn't mind having them called dainty, and she didn't mind letting the peddler help her up onto the seat, and she didn't mind at all riding beside him back to the cabin with his shoulder rubbing against hers as the wagon swayed.

Well, Hanna's mother and father were so taken by the young

man they wanted to buy every single notion in his wagon, the bolts of calico and sacks of herbs, the nails and windowpanes and iron pots. The trouble was, they had no money, and wouldn't have any until the tobacco was harvested and cured and sold.

"Then I'll just wait for harvest," said the peddler.

And he did. Every morning he rose before dawn and went rattling away to sell his notions in the hills and hollows around Old Smoky, and every night he rolled back into the dooryard, where he slept in his wagon. Hanna never heard the wagon leave without fearing he wouldn't come back, but he did come back, time and again, all that summer and into the fall.

In the evenings he sat in the cabin and told stories that made her ache to see the world. "That young man's voice goes down just as slick as sugar water," said her mother. Her father said, "He's been about everywhere there is, from the sound of it." Later, when the old folks fell asleep, Hanna and the peddler went for walks in the dusty moonlight, through a whisper of crickets, and he never ran short of sweet things to say. To hear him talk, she was the loveliest woman God had ever made, from her toes to the wisps of her hair. She believed only about half of what he said, but she took pleasure in hearing it all.

On Sundays, when he did not go selling, the peddler helped Hanna catch up on her chores, pounding loose shakes back onto the roof, turning manure onto the garden, currying the horses.

Before long Hanna's mother and father were calling him "your young man," and by the coming of cool weather Hanna was beginning to think of him as her own man for good and true. She imagined they would get married, build a new house next to her mother and father's cabin, string some fences and raise sheep, add some beef cattle, more hogs, more hens, turn that mountaintop farm into a regular paradise.

Harvest time came. He worked right beside her, pulling tobacco leaves, sewing them together by the stems, hanging them on poles in the barn loft. The work barely crawled along. It seemed like his fingers kept getting entangled with hers. He kept thinking of news to whisper into her ear. Every little while, whispering, their lips drifted closer and closer until they kissed, and work had to wait. Still he said nothing about marriage. He talked about everything under the sun, called her every manner of tender thing, but never mentioned marriage.

Hanging in the barn, the tobacco leaves turned from green to yellow, from yellow to biscuit, from biscuit to the dark chocolate shade of old harness.

One morning Hanna and her peddler climbed into the barn loft to sniff the tobacco and judge its color.

"Look's to me like that's ready for market," he said.

"It looks prime and pretty to me," Hanna agreed. "Time to haul it on down to town and see what we can get for it."

"My wagon's about empty, I done sold so many of my notions." He laid a finger under her chin. "Why don't you and me load it up and go sell that crop and take the money and set us up in a house somewhere?"

Hanna laughed, but there was a little fear in her laughter. "What're you saying?"

"I'm saying, let's go off and get married."

"Off where?"

The peddler gestured out through the window of the loft. "Off this blame mountain. New Orleans, maybe, or Memphis, Atlanta, Charleston. Some place where they've got streets and lights and enough people to where you can sell your stuff without riding half a day between cabins."

Hanna filled up with a longing to go. "I never lived any place but up here on Old Smoky."

"You never lived at all till I come along, did you, sugar?"

The finger under her chin felt like a point of fire. His lips were sliding toward hers. A thought made her hesitate. "Wouldn't it be hard on my folks to move like that, old and ailing the way they are?"

"Who said anything about taking them along?"

A sudden coldness shot through her. "Did you just figure on *leaving* them?"

"Why, sure. They'd get by."

"You think *I'd* leave them?"

"To go away with me, you would, now wouldn't you?"

The peddler slipped a hand around her back, but Hanna spun free, stumbled across the loft, and glared at him. "Well, if that's what you think," she said, "you got another think coming."

The peddler sidled after her, a handsome man, his thicket of hair curly and dark, his voice like a creek over stones. "Now, sugar, you know you'll come along with me. When's the next man going to roll by? Such a pretty woman! You don't want to nurse two old folks away up here in the middle of nowhere, all alone, an old maid with fingers wore down to the nub."

Hanna backed away from him, thinking, *I do want to go, I do I do,* but shaking her head no.

"Who's going to buy shoes for your dainty little feet?" he whispered. "Who's going to put gloves on your hands?"

She kept shaking her head, backing.

"Sure, you'll come," he murmured.

"No!" Hanna cried, and it tore her up to say it.

At last the peddler let out a hiss of exasperation. "Well, then, just stay here and dry up like an old gourd. There's other women on my road."

He turned away. Hanna reached out, laid a hand on his shoulder. "Feed your horses before you go."

"They ain't hungry. They already been fed."

"Then grease your wagon, if you're really going so far."

"It's already been greased." He shrugged free of her hand, went swinging down the ladder.

"Say goodbye to my folks," Hanna called after him. "They dote on you."

He called back, "You tell them, sugar. I got places to go."

Through the window of the loft Hanna watched him leap onto the wagon seat, give the reins a flick, and roll away. After a moment he began singing in an angry voice. For a long while she could see and hear him as he wound along the snaky mountain road, and then he rolled down through a cloud and disappeared, gone, gone, and all that remained was the ache and dwindling fire of his singing.

The Blue-Tail Fly

[TRADITIONAL]

When I was young I used to wait
On massa and hand him the plate,
And pass the bottle when he got dry,
And brush away the blue-tail fly.

Jimmy, crack corn, and I don't care,
Jimmy, crack corn, and I don't care,
Jimmy, crack corn, and I don't care,
My massa's gone away!

And when he'd ride in the afternoon
I'd follow after with a hickory broom,
The pony being very shy,
When bitten by the blue-tail fly.

One day when riding round the farm,
The flies so numerous they did swarm,
One chanced to bite him on the thigh,
The Devil take the blue-tail fly!

The pony run, he jump, he kick,
He throwed old massa in the ditch,
He died and the jury wondered why,
The verdict was, the blue-tail fly!

We laid him under a persimmon tree,
His epitaph was there to see,
"Beneath this stone I'm forced to lie—
Victim of a blue-tail fly."

Old massa's dead and gone to rest,
They say all things is for the best.
I'll never forget till the day I die,
Old massa and the blue-tail fly.

The hornet gets in eyes and nose,
The skeeter bites you through your clothes,
The gallinipper flies up high,
But worst of all, the blue-tail fly.

You know, whenever Massa wanted anything, day or night, he sent for his slave-boy, Jimmy. Massa might take a hunger along about two hours before daylight, and he'd yell for Jimmy to fetch him a pecan pie. Or he might get an itch on his backbone and he'd holler for Jimmy to come scratch it. Mornings, he liked to look over his land and watch his darkies working, so Jimmy always curried and saddled the red pony and had it waiting by the door when Massa stepped outside. Massa didn't trust horses, they were too big and wild, so he rode ahead on the pony; Jimmy rode behind on a mule, carrying a hickory broom to brush the flies away from the pony's rump.

Jimmy slept in the kitchen, when he slept at all. While Cook was fixing food for the white folks, he snitched nibbles for himself. Breakfast, dinner, and supper, dressed up in a bleached coat that smelled of lye, he carried plates and bottles from the kitchen to the dining room. While the white folks ate, Jimmy stood behind Massa's chair and swung a fan over Massa's balding head to keep away the flies. Indoors or out, Massa hated flies. Then after the white folks finished their meal, Jimmy cleared off the table and ate every scrap they left behind; but still he never could put on any fat, he was run so ragged.

Massa put on fat just fine. He sure could murder the groceries. And he was even worse on the drinkables. In an evening he could swallow enough whiskey to pickle a hog. "Crack corn," is what he called it. "Jimmy! You, Jimmy!" he'd yell before bedtime, "I'm plumb out of crack corn. Run fetch me another jug." Most nights it took both Jimmy and a house-girl named Caroline to heave Massa into bed. They rolled him on his back and took off his shoes and hung a tent of gauzy linen over him to keep off the mosquitoes. The two of them would get their eyes tangled up, looking at one another across the white man's wheezing body, waiting for him to drift off. Before you knew it, Massa was snoring like a saw-mill.

But Massa hardly ever sawed straight through until morning. He was troubled by bitter dreams. Once or twice before dawn he would sit up in bed, yelling for Jimmy. And Jimmy would come running in, with his eyelids propped open, and say, "What's ailing you, Massa?"

"I dreamed my cotton went up in flames!" Massa might answer, or, "I dreamed my darkies all run off!" or, "I dreamed a flood lifted this mansion right off its cellar hole and carried it away down the Mississippi and dumped it in the Gulf of Mexico!"

"Ain't none of that happen, Massa," Jimmy would say. "Everything just like it always was."

Such lullabies soothed Massa back to sleep. He made so much ruckus, snoring and yelling, that Missis moved her bed on down to the far end of the house. She had her beauty to look after. There wasn't a thing in the world harder on a woman's looks, she would tell you, than tossing and turning all the night.

Sleeplessness wasn't harming Jimmy's looks any, to Caroline's way of seeing. She thought he was just about the cat's meow, he was so handsome. She cut her eyes at him every time she had a chance, in between running errands here, there, and yonder for Missis.

The hardest job Caroline had to do was telling Missis what a beautiful lady she was.

"Do you notice any wrinkles starting around my eyes, Caroline?" Missis might say.

And Caroline would have to answer, "Lord, no, Missis, your face is smooth as a new peach!"

"Do you think my waist is just a wee bit fuller than it used to be?"

"Why, Missis, it's so narrow, I don't see how it keeps your top up off your bottom!"

Every time Missis frowned at herself in the mirror, Caroline had to say, "My, my, don't you look prettier than sunrise this morning, Missis! Ain't your hair as shiny as gold! Don't your skin look like a magnolia blossom!" To tell the truth, Caroline thought the white lady's face looked more like the ash-colored sow in the pig-lot; but truth was too strong for telling.

In the early mornings, before Massa and Missis were up, Caroline and Jimmy sat in the kitchen talking silly talk while Cook banged together breakfast. He called her Honey and she called him Molasses, and their talk got so sweet, Cook said a person could pour it over pancakes.

Well, time went on, and Massa's head grew as bald as a baby's hind end, and Missis went to smearing egg whites on her face every night to keep away the wrinkles, and Jimmy and Caroline got on up late in their teen age. By and by they settled on getting married. One night they went down to the shacks where the field slaves lived. Everybody circled around, and the oldest woman and the oldest man hobbled into the center of the ring and held both ends of a broom. Jimmy and Caroline hooked hands and jumped over that broom, with all the brothers and sisters looking on, and when they hit the ground they were married.

Back in the kitchen, where Cook treated them with corn bread broken up in sweet milk, Caroline asked Jimmy, "We going to tell Massa and Missis?"

"I don't see where it's any of their business if we're married or we ain't married," he said.

So at night they laid their pallets side by side on the kitchen floor and wrapped themselves in a single quilt. Now and again Jimmy would get up to fetch a jug for Massa or soothe him through a bitter dream or catch mosquitoes that were pestering him. Now and again Caroline would go sing for Missis when the white lady couldn't sleep.

Caroline grew so weary from traipsing back and forth in the middle of the night, and so grumpy from humoring the Missis, that she forgot to dull the edge on her tongue.

One evening Missis was getting dressed for a fancy ball. She suddenly turned on Caroline and said, "What should I wear?"

Caroline was bone-tired. Her eyes felt like they'd been used to scrub the floor. She looked out the window and muttered, "How about you wear a horse saddle?"

"What's that you say? Speak up, child."

"I says, how about you start with a corset?"

"That goes without saying, child. Here, lace me up."

Lacing the Missis into a corset was a job for three strong men with crowbars, not one spindly girl with sore fingers. Caroline tugged and yanked and huffed, but she couldn't squeeze that white lady thin enough to fit her inside the ball gown.

"Come, now, you're not trying," Missis complained.

"I'm trying, I'm trying. You like a sausage."

"A what?"

"I say, you like a *corsage*. A bunch of gardenias, you so pretty."

"How sweet," said Missis. "I do think the egg whites are working wonders for my skin."

"I wonder every time I look at you," Caroline agreed. "Wonder and wonder."

"And of course a lady must avoid the sun to preserve her paleness."

"Oh, Lord! I never seen such pale! Why, you as white as the underside of a maggot."

"A *what?*"

"*Magnolia*, Missy. You as white as the underside of a magnolia."

"Here, now," said Missis, "I'll hold my breath and you see if you can't pull those laces a teensy bit tighter."

Caroline pulled for all she was worth, but still there was too much Missis to squeeze inside the dancing dress. She let out a hiss between her teeth, and said, "You ought to be greased and slid in with a shoehorn."

"Ought to be pleased about what?" said Missis.

By now Caroline was too worn out and frazzled to lie. "I didn't say nothing about *pleased*. I said *greased*. Roll you in hog lard, and then maybe you slip inside your dress, but you so too big for it the buttons popping liable to kill chickens in the yard, and the tightness of it liable to shove all the wrinkles on your whole body into your face so you look like a dead whale that's done washed all the way across the ocean and got half eaten up with salt . . ."

Caroline had a lot more to say, but she quit when Missis started screaming for Massa.

Massa came running, one foot in his dancing shoe and one

foot bare, and he took out his belt right then and whipped Caroline until she cried for mercy.

After the white folks rode off to another plantation for their fancy ball, Jimmy rubbed Caroline's back with butter. "Now you done it," he said.

"Now I done it," she agreed.

"He going to sell you down to New Orleans, I bet."

"I don't doubt it."

"I hope a tree falls on them before they get home."

"Now who got the sharp tongue?" said Caroline.

"I'm only saying like I feel. I hope they both get struck by lightning. I hope a pack of wild boars come out of the bayous and run plumb over them. I hope a swarm of bees land on their heads. I hope a cyclone pick them up off their buggy and set them down in the Pacific Ocean."

Next morning, Massa and Missis slept in late. Cook grumbled that she would have to feed them dinner for breakfast if they didn't move their bones pretty quick. After a while, Massa started hacking and coughing and growling up in his bedroom, and pretty soon his feet hit the floor. Word came downstairs that Missis was laid too low with upset and mortification to leave her room. Another girl from the slave quarters was to come wait on her, and Caroline was to go out and chop weeds in the field. Jimmy and Caroline gave one another the broody eye. Worse trouble coming.

Cook said to Caroline, "If I was you, girl, I'd make myself scarce for a while. Else Massa gone whup you again soon as he see you."

"Me and my mouth," Caroline sighed. She gave Jimmy a

fat kiss on the lips, saying, "I see you after dark, sweetling." She turned up her dress to get it off her ankles, tied up her hair, and trudged on out to the cotton field.

Watching her go, Jimmy ached way down deep in his marrow.

Cook said, "Jimmy, you got a face on you mean enough to slam doors. You best slap on a smile before Massa come down."

It was almost noon when Massa staggered outside and climbed onto his pony. His face was the color of a baked apple. Jimmy rode behind him on the mule, as usual, with the hickory broom over his shoulder to use for brushing the flies away. He looked at Massa's back and thought of the lash marks on Caroline.

"Jimmy," said Massa, "you people are a deep mystery to me."

"Yes sir."

"You don't seem to have a drop of gratitude in your hearts."

"No sir."

"Here we take you into our own home, treat you with every kindness, and what do we get in return? Hatred and insults."

"Yes sir."

"You take that girl, Caroline. She's got a tongue on her like a buggy whip. After years of pampering, was she thankful to my wife? Was she respectful?"

"I expect not," said Jimmy.

"No, indeed, she wasn't. Not one little bit. She said things so cruel my wife won't even repeat them to me. Well, that girl has said her last say under my roof. She's going on the block. I don't care if she only brings ten dollars, I'm going to sell her."

Jimmy didn't trust himself to answer. He and Massa rode on through the cotton rows, then drew up beside the bent-over field hands who were chopping weeds. Caroline was huddled in the midst of them, but kept her face turned away. Seeing her there in the dust and heat, thinking of her being sold on the auction block, Jimmy felt woozy with anger. The sun blistered down. Massa sat in his white suit on his red pony, watching his darkies stoop. It was so hot, the only living things that stirred, aside from the slaves, were the blue-tail flies. They buzzed and whined around Massa.

"Where are you at with that broom, Jimmy?" said Massa.

Jimmy gave a halfhearted sweep. It was the same broom he and Caroline had jumped over to get married. He gripped it now as if it were an ax, and glared at the back of Massa's head.

The flies kept buzzing in circles. One of them landed on the pony's rump. Jimmy lifted the broom to swat it away, but he held up, and in a split second the fly bit the pony, the pony kicked up its hind legs and swished its tail, Massa went flying into the ditch and landed smack on his head. He lay there all crumpled and still. The field hands straightened up to stare.

"Massa?" said Jimmy.

But Massa was dead as a shovel from a broken neck.

Everybody figured Jimmy's own neck would be broken pretty soon by a noose. The sheriff put him in jail to wait for trial. "What did I do?" Jimmy protested. "Can I help it if he rode a shy pony?"

The Missis was so heart-struck, she wanted her familiar old Caroline back up at the house to look after her. "I'll forgive you, child," said Missis, "if you promise never to say an unkind word to me again."

Caroline crossed her fingers and promised. Every night she stole over to the jail to whisper with Jimmy through the window of his cell. What they whispered was so feverish with love, it's a wonder they didn't melt the bars.

Before too long the judge rode back through town and held a trial. The jury leaned forward in their chairs and listened while Jimmy told what had happened. When he came to describe how the fly landed on the pony's rump and how he couldn't sweep the broom down fast enough, the judge interrupted him. "What kind of fly did you say that was?"

"Blue-tail, Your Honor," said Jimmy.

The men on the jury nodded their heads. Everyone there had been bitten many a time. They knew no hand on earth was as quick as that fly. The jurors rubbed old sores on their arms, on the backs of their necks, on their knees. And when it came time for a verdict, they pronounced Jimmy innocent and laid all the blame on that blue-tail fly.

Drill, Ye Tarriers, Drill

[TRADITIONAL]

Every morning at seven o'clock,
There's twenty tarriers a-working on the rock.
Boss comes along and he says, "Keep still,
And come down heavy on your cast-iron drills."

> *And drill, ye tarriers, drill,*
> *Drill, ye tarriers, drill.*
> *O it's work all day for the sugar in your tay,*
> *Down behind the railway,*
> *And drill, ye tarriers, drill!*
> *And blast! And fire!*

Our new foreman is Gene McCann,
By God, he is a blame mean man.
Last week a premature blast went off
And a mile in the air went big Jim Goff.

Next time payday come around,
Jim Goff a dollar short was found.
When asked what for, came this reply,
"You was docked for the time you was up in the sky."

Boss is a fine man down to the ground,
He married a lady six foot round.
She bakes good bread and she bakes it well,
But she bakes it hard as the holes in Hell.

You may search high and low and wear out your eyes with looking, but you will never find a stingier skin-flint of a man than Gene McCann. If you asked the gang of Irish tarriers who worked for him laying down track on the Chesapeake and Ohio Railroad, they would tell you he was the hardest boss to come along since Moses drove the Israelites across the desert. Stumble to the roadbed at seven o'clock, with your eyes still bleary and your arms feeling like bags of sand from sleep, and Gene McCann would already be there, barking at you: "Come on, lads, stir your bones! Come on! Have you forgotten overnight how to lift a hammer? Have those shovels sprouted roots so you can't get them off the ground? Dig, lads, *dig!*" And if you survived until sundown, there McCann would still be, keeping you after dark to lay one last rail and straighten out spikes by lantern light.

On his account the tarriers renamed the C & O the Cheap and Ornery. They couldn't outwit him, because he was as Irish as they were. Any dodge they tried for getting out of work, he saw right through it. "I was there when the Devil invented loafing," he bragged. It was no use complaining of a sore back, because McCann did not believe in aches and pains. "What's a body for, I ask you, but hefting and heaving?" And they couldn't scorn him for being a straw boss, either, since he sweated right alongside them. He sharpened their cast-iron drills, fitted new hickory handles in their picks, delivered wagonloads of rails, tamped black powder in the blasting holes, lifted and grunted and did whatever needed doing to keep them all hard at it. Working under him you never could slow down, for he sang the hammer songs faster and louder than any other boss on the railroad.

"Ach, but you're a hard man, Gene McCann," the tarriers would grumble.

"And why shouldn't I be?" he would answer. "The family I come from was so poor my father kept our only potato under his pillow. When my dear mother made soup she dipped a bone on a string into boiling water, let it soak there half a minute on weekdays and a full minute on Sunday before she pulled it out. Once we came by a bit of salt fish and lived two weeks off the smell of it. If any mice were fool enough to come nosing for scraps under our table, we had mouse stew. The last winter I was in Ireland we burned our chairs to keep warm. Tell me now, why shouldn't I be a hard man?"

At night the tarriers sat around in the shanties and told stories on their boss: Gene McCann is so tight with his money, when he wears out his boot soles he turns them over and uses the other side. He hangs onto a silver dollar so long, the eagle's feathers turn white and fall out, and McCann stuffs them in his mattress. Once he trained a penny to jump back in his pocket when he whistled, and don't you know he spent that same penny two dozen times. When things are slow, he lays off the hands on his watch, to keep from having to pay them. If he were the sun, he'd charge the moon rent for using the sky at night. Why, McCann even married a fat woman, to get more wife for the price of his wedding license.

The wife was named Molly, six foot high and six foot around, come over the ocean from a boggy farm outside Limerick, and she cooked grub for the railroad gang. She had her strong points, but cooking wasn't one of them. The tarriers swore she ground up cinders to use for pepper. When they ate her pies, they kept their eyes closed, for fear of what might turn up at the end of the fork. They found horsehairs in their beef. Her chicken tasted mighty like possum, and the bacon like fried snake. If you didn't keep a hand on her biscuits, the weevils would carry them off and lay them up for a fortress to hide in. You could drive nails with her cakes, and her sourdough bread would do for crossties.

It wasn't her fault she fed them such measly fare. Gene McCann had a contract for the food, and he didn't believe in paying any more than he had to for it. When he went to market he took his gun along, figuring to shoot a meal here and there, sometimes in the woods, sometimes in a barnyard nobody was watching. Whatever he saved by scrimping on food went in his own pocket. The way he looked at it, so long as his men could work all day without keeling over, they were eating just fine. "You don't want to eat too high on the hog," he warned them, "or you'll spoil your belly, and when the hard times come how will you get by?"

The tarriers had all known harder times back in Ireland. They knew the taste of boiled shoe leather. They knew how hungry you get on a diet of wind. So they ate whatever Molly McCann served them, did whatever work Gene McCann told them to do, and kept mum. Here at least there was a coal fire in the bunkhouse and a shirt on your back and sugar for your tea. In America you didn't have to pay tithes to the church or taxes to the great lord. Nobody would hang you for standing on your hind legs and speaking your mind. If you worked hard, one day you might become a foreman yourself, might even buy your own railway company and ride all over the country in a silver-plated Pullman car. Hadn't Gene Mc-Cann himself started out pushing a wheelbarrow? Dreaming of ease, the tarriers swung their hammers and shovels, and envied their boss for having already climbed one rung above them on the ladder of riches.

The owners of the line were pleased with their hard-nosed foreman. They paid him bonuses for laying down more track than any other gang boss on the Chesapeake and Ohio. In flat country his crew made five or seven miles a day. Rough country slowed them down, but still they cut through hills and bridged over creeks fast enough to make the owners smile.

His crew also lost men at a great rate. Some died of the heat, some in rock slides, some from explosions. In West Virginia a tunnel caved in on three men. In Kentucky a bridge collapsed and dropped two others into the Licking River. Gene McCann hated to see it, what a pity, such good lads. Ach, he thought, you could have built quite a stretch of railway over the bodies of Irishmen. But there it was. You did a job of work and you paid the price. And besides, whenever a lad fell, here came another husky one fresh from Ireland to take his place. No good looking behind when a whole country lay before you, and all of it crying for railroads.

Oh, he was a hard man, that Gene McCann. How hard? The tarriers would tell you about the time when big Jim Goff was pouring powder down a drill hole, scuffed his boot on the rock and threw a spark, and BAM! the blast went off, drove big Jim about a mile in the air, and all the while he was up there Gene McCann kept studying his watch, and next time payday rolled around big Jim come up a dollar short, and he says to McCann, "Why for?" and McCann says, "You was docked for the time you was up in the sky."

The owners of the C & O admired McCann's attitude. They kept giving him raises, put him in charge of bigger and bigger gangs. Pretty soon he was bossing the whole construction crew, from Virginia all the way to Ohio. He had to ride an express train just to get a look at all his men. Before you knew it he was wearing a white shirt and carrying a logbook, and never dirtying his hands on a prybar or hammer. By and by he rose to vice president. He lived among papers. Closing his eyes at night, he saw nothing but numbers. The only time he stirred from his office was to celebrate the opening of a new road. When he stopped by the section of the line where his old gang was working, they looked at him with his tall silk hat and clean fingernails and face the color of new cheese, and they could not think what to say. As for Gene McCann, he was too busy checking on the progress of the railway to spend time chewing fat with a raggedy bunch of Irish tarriers.

John Henry

[TRADITIONAL]

When John Henry was a little baby,
You could hold him in the palm of your hand,
He gave a long and a lonesome cry,
Said, "Steel be the death of me, Lawd, Lawd,
Steel be the death of me."

They took John Henry to the mountain,
That mountain was so high,
Mountain so tall and John Henry so small,
That he laid down his hammer and he cried, Lawd, Lawd,
Laid down his hammer and he cried.

Captain says to John Henry,
Says, "I believe this mountain's sinking in."
Says, "Stand back, captain, and doncha be afraid,
It's nothing but my hammer sucking wind, Lawd, Lawd,
Nothing but my hammer sucking wind."

Captain told John Henry,
"Gonna bring my steam drill round,
Gonna take my steam drill out on the job,
Gonna beat John Henry down, Lawd, Lawd,
Gonna beat John Henry down."

John Henry says to the captain,
"A man ain't nothing but a man,
And before I let that steam drill beat me down,
I'll die with my hammer in my hand, Lawd, Lawd,
Die with my hammer in my hand."

John Henry spoke to his shaker,
Says, "Shaker, why don't you sing?
I'm throwing nine pounds from my hips on down,
Just listen to the cold steel ring, Lawd, Lawd,
Listen to the cold steel ring."

John Henry he told his captain,
"Looky yonder, there, what do I see?
Your drill's done broke and your hole's done choke,
And you can't drive steel like me, Lawd, Lawd,
Can't drive steel like me."

John Henry hammering on the right-hand side,
Steam drill driving on the left,
John Henry beat that steam drill down,
But he hammered his fool self to death, Lawd, Lawd,
Hammered his fool self to death.

John Henry hammering in the mountain,
Till the handle of his hammer caught on fire,
He drove so hard till he broke his poor heart,
Then he laid down his hammer and he died, Lawd, Lawd,
Laid down his hammer and he died.

Women in the west heard of John Henry's death,
They couldn't hardly stay in bed,
Stood in the rain, flagged that east-bound train,
"Going where that man fell dead, Lawd, Lawd,
Going where that man fell dead."

They took John Henry to the tunnel,
And they buried him in the sand.
And every locomotive comes a-rolling by,
Says, "There lies a steel-driving man, Lawd, Lawd,
There lies a steel-driving man."

Now some say he come from England
And some say he come from Spain,
But I say he's nothing but a Louisiana man,
Leader of a steel-driving gang, Lawd, Lawd,
Leader of a steel-driving gang.

When John Henry was still so little you could hold him in the palm of your hand, his momma gave him a cup, his poppa gave him a spoon, and he started in to hammering. He made their hut on that Louisiana plantation sound like the engine room on a steamboat. Poppa would shout over the noise, "If I don't miss my bet, that boy's going to be a bruiser."

When John Henry was just about knee-high, he loved to climb on his momma's lap to ask her about mountains, and on his poppa's lap to ask him about railroads.

"You be pure Africa," his momma said, "and over in Africa the land rumple up and down. Trees bristle on the hills like hairs on the back of a hound." Here in Louisiana on the black skirts of the Mississippi River, the land stretched out flat as a griddle, and the trees stood so far apart that a boy could die of sunstroke running between one patch of shade and the next. There were miles and miles of cotton, but a boy couldn't hide under a cotton bush.

"Building railroads," his poppa told him, "they take and lay down these crossties, and they lay down tracks, and the engines chug here and yonder, wherever they take a mind to go. If they come to a river, they build themselves a bridge. Come to a hill, they knock that hill flat. Come to a mountain, why, they drill a hole plumb through."

Such talk gave John Henry the shivers. He would listen all day in the blacksmith shop while Poppa hammered shoes for the Master's horses and talked about the wide world. He would listen to Momma at night when she came back to the hut, all wheezy and droopy-eyed, from cleaning the Master's house. Snuggling in for sleep, John Henry didn't hear the rustle of his cornhusk pallet, didn't hear the crickets, didn't hear the river's grumble. What he heard as he drifted off was the croon of Momma's voice and the ring of Poppa's hammer.

John Henry took a castoff hoe and scraped the dirt of the dooryard into a hill. He patted it hard with his feet and hands. Then he beat on the cup with the spoon, to make the racket of men drilling holes in rock, and he dug a tunnel through. Crawling under his mountain he whistled and roared. Momma cried out when she heard him, "Train a-coming!" Poppa yelled, "Clear the track!"

Soon John Henry stood higher than the bow on Momma's apron, higher than the buckle on Poppa's belt. "Time you come lend me a hand," Poppa said, and he taught John Henry how to pull the red-hot iron from the forge and douse it in the water tub, how to pump the bellows, how to make the anvil ring.

By and by, news reached Louisiana about war breaking out between the North and the South. At night, in the darkness of the hut, John Henry listened to Momma and Poppa whispering about Mr. Lincoln and freedom. All the while he kept stretching up taller, kept swelling out wider. The muscles in his arm, thick from hammering, jumped and squirmed like pigs in a sack. When he grew tall enough to eat soup off his momma's head, strangers began dropping by the blacksmith shop to look him over, white men who stared with the cold eyes of catfish. They murmured to one another about money and blood. Poppa gave them looks sharper than horseshoe nails.

One evening Momma came home from the Big House to say the Master had sold John Henry for a thousand dollars. "Man coming to get him tomorrow," said Momma.

"No, he don't," Poppa said.

"Not while I breathe," Momma agreed. Her apron was full of bread and ham from the Master's kitchen.

That very night they headed north, following the Big Dipper, north toward the mountains and the railroads. John Henry felt as if he'd swallowed a red-hot coal, he was so burning with fear, especially when the dogs howled behind them. The three of them slept curled together in barns, in hollow trees, under the ledges of creeks. They ate rabbits, berries, roots. The miles were long and fearful. Momma took a fever in Tennessee, and died of it in Kentucky. Poppa made it all the way to the banks of the Ohio, where he asked a lone white man for a ride across the river. The man's eyes got big and his mouth split open. "Runaway slave!" he yelled. Poppa swung around and set off running, but the man pulled a gun and fired.

John Henry hid in the bushes, watching his poppa die. After a while, five white men came and hauled the body away in a wagon. John Henry listened with his eyes squeezed shut until the wheels rattled beyond hearing. Then he dove into the river. Weighted down with miseries, he didn't try to swim, didn't try to float, just gave himself to the water. He sank to the bottom, touched the mud with his toes, and rose back up. He sank again, rose again, sank and rose. After bobbing up three times he knew he wasn't meant to drown, and so he swam across the river to the free soil of Indiana.

As soon as he came to a railbed, all shiny with fresh ribbons of steel, he followed it north until he reached the gang who were laying new track. The captain of the gang took one look at John Henry's shoulders, gave him a nine-pound hammer and a bucket of spikes, and jumped back out of the way to let him work. Three Irishmen drove spikes on one rail, and John Henry hammered all by his lonesome on the other, but still he pulled ahead. The men bedding down crossties and laying rails huffed and grunted, trying to keep ahead of him. "Slow down, big fellow, or you'll bust a gut," they called to him. But John Henry knew only one way to move, and that was full speed ahead.

From the day John Henry stripped off his shirt and picked up that nine-pound hammer, he said goodbye to loneliness. Every town the railroad gang passed through, the girls leaned out the windows to stare. It didn't matter which part of John Henry they took a gander at first—shoulders, hands, back as broad as a kitchen table, face handsomer than a Pharaoh's— they liked what they saw. They waved their bonnets at him and brought him cakes wrapped in perfumed scarves. Pretty, pretty, pretty big man, they sang to him from doorways.

The people of Indianapolis heard the ring of his hammer from a mile away. Not long after, folks heard him in Fort Wayne, Chicago, Toledo, Cleveland. In all those stretches of country, there were few hills higher than the one John Henry had scraped together in his dooryard years ago. Tired of all this flat country, he said to the captain, "Where's these mountains at?" The captain said, "You wait till we get to Pennsylvania."

Pennsylvania looked as good to John Henry as the Africa he carried in his mind. The land rumpled up and down like the quilt on a feverish bed. Every few miles there was a river to bridge, a hill to lay low, a mountain to dig through. John Henry put a hammer on his shoulder and shouted at the mountains, "You might as well split open now, babe, because a man's coming at you." He swung that hammer from his hips on down, two hundred and twenty-five pounds of him, and drove six-foot drills into the rock of Pennsylvania. A shaker man held the drill and gave it a turn after each lick of John Henry's hammer. When they were done, a blaster man tamped the hole full of black powder and blew the rock to bits.

John Henry's crew drilled and blasted through Pennsylvania into Maryland, through Maryland into West Virginia, on their way to Washington. Mr. Lincoln had been killed and the slaves had been set free, but John Henry still thought of Washington as Mr. Lincoln's city. He wanted to lay track right up to the steps of the White House and go say hello to whatever President lived there now. "A man come calling," he would say, and shake the President's hand.

But first there was a West Virginia mountain standing in the way. Big Bend they called it, and the tunnel through it would be a mile and a quarter long, the longest on earth. John Henry greased the handle on his hammer with tallow and started in swinging. He swung so hard, the blacksmith had to sharpen his drills every hour, and the shakers had to take turns holding for him. He swung so fast, the sound of the hammerhead sucking wind was like the panting of a giant.

They were halfway through the Big Bend Tunnel when the captain came up to John Henry one morning and said, "Move over, I got a newfangled steam drill here I want to try, drills faster than any three men alive."

John Henry took a squint at this engine. It looked like a midget locomotive broken out in a rash of wheels and belts and valves. He spat. "Ain't no machine made can outdrill me."

"Bet you a month's pay," said the captain. "You against the steam drill for half an hour tomorrow morning."

"You got a bet," said John Henry. "Just bring me a twenty-pound hammer, a good fresh shaker, and half a dozen hard-steel drills."

Next morning the railway bosses rode down from Pittsburgh to watch the contest, and the track-laying gang crowded into the tunnel. It was hot in the mountain, and the air was thick. John Henry wore nothing but patched britches. Even before he started swinging, he gleamed with sweat, like coal in the rain. He filled his chest with air. The steam drill hissed. Everyone hushed. Then the captain pulled out his pocket watch and shouted, "Go!"

It was bedlam in the mountain, the hammer ringing, steam drill pounding, bosses rooting for the engine, crewmen hollering for the man.

"Show them how, John Henry!"

The engine wheezed and clanked and whammed. John Henry's muscles swelled up, his veins stood out, steam rose off his back.

"Drive it down, John Henry!"

Watching him, the crewmen thought of tornadoes, thunderheads, the Mississippi River on a rampage.

"Let it fly, John Henry!"

Even the bosses dropped their jaws when they saw him swing. The captain watched the machine with a frown on his face. He let the time run over, hoping John Henry would tucker out. But after thirty-five minutes the engine threw a gear. "Stop!" yelled the captain. They measured the holes. John Henry had drilled fourteen feet, and the steam drill had only made nine.

The crewmen cheered. "Machine got whupped by a man!"

"Give me water," panted John Henry. "Stand out of my way and give me air."

They brought him a bucket of water, fanned him with their shirts. When his breath came silky again, the gang lifted him onto their shoulders and carried him to the railroad camp, a load of muscle, a load of heart, and every crewman reached up to put a hand on his wet body. John Henry never let go of the hammer, not even when they set him down on his pallet.

"You done seen it," he told them.

"We seen it and we ain't never going to forget," the gang answered.

Then John Henry eased himself down, slipped away to sleep, and never came back.

The next one to touch him—cold cold—was the doctor, who told the crowd gathered round the fallen man, "He burst a vessel in his head."

Word of John Henry's death traveled east and west, north

and south, everywhere the railroads ran. White and black, men lay down their tools, women put on their party dresses, bright as birds, and from ten states around they hurried to the Big Bend Tunnel to see this man go down with a twenty-pound hammer into his giant's hole in the rock.

Casey Jones

[TRADITIONAL]

Come all you rounders, for I want you to hear,
The story of a brave engineer.
Casey Jones was the rounder's name,
On a big eight-wheeler of a mighty frame.

Casey Jones, he pushed on the throttle,
Casey Jones was a brave engineer,
Come on, Casey, and blow the whistle,
Blow the whistle so they all can hear.

Caller called Casey at half-past four,
He kissed his wife at the station door,
Climbed to the cab with the orders in his hand,
Says, "This is my trip to the Holy Land."

Out of South Memphis yard on the fly,
Heard the fireman say, "You got a white eye."
Well, the switchmen knew by the engine moan
That the man at the throttle was Casey Jones.

The rain was coming down five or six weeks,
The railroad track was like the bed of a creek.
They slowed her down to a thirty-mile gait,
And the south-bound mail was eight hours late.

Firemen says, "Casey, you're running too fast,
You run the blackboard, last station you passed."
Casey says, "I believe we'll make it though,
For she steams a lot better than I ever know."

Casey says, "Fireman, don't you fret,
Keep knocking at the fire door, don't give up yet,
I'm going to run her till she leaves the rail,
Or make it on time with the south-bound mail."

Around the curve and down the dump,
Two locomotives was bound to jump,
Fireman hollered, "Casey, it's just ahead,
We might jump and make it but we'll wind up dead."

Around the curve comes a passenger train,
Her headlight was shining in his eyes through the rain,
Casey blew the whistle, a mighty blast,
But the locomotive was coming too fast.

The locomotives met in the middle of the hill,
In a head-on tangle that was bound to kill.
He tried to do his duty, the yardmen said,
But Casey Jones was scalded dead.

Well, Casey Jones was all right.
He stuck by his duty day and night.
They loved his whistle and his ring number three,
And he came into Memphis on the old I.C.

Headaches and heartaches and all kinds of pain,
They ain't apart from a railroad train.
Stories of brave men, noble and grand,
Belong to the life of a railroad man.

Any night of his childhood, Casey Jones could lie in bed and listen to steamboats on the Mississippi hooting at one another and mule skinners on the road hollering at their teams. But those were poky sounds, old sounds, nothing to get excited about. Grandpa could have heard the same when he was a boy. The sound that roused Casey up from his pillow and drew him to the window and set him atingle was a new one, a fast one, the long wolfish howl of a locomotive barreling down the track. Hearing it, he always wanted to go jump on a train and ride to the ends of the earth. The only pleasure he could imagine greater than riding behind an iron horse was driving one. Glory, glory, he thought, to have all that power in your hands!

Casey did his listening and longing down in the western tip of Kentucky, where that state kicks a toe into the side of Arkansas. It was a country of swervy roads and crooked rivers, but the railways ran straight as the eyebeams of God. They sliced through hills, flung trestles over valleys, as if to say they had places to go and no time to dawdle.

Every chance he got, Casey stole down to the Mobile and Ohio tracks. Just gazing north or south along the empty glittering lines was enough to fill him with yearning. Long before a train was due he could lay his ear against the rail and hear the ring of steel approaching. When he spied smoke, he jumped back onto the gravel and watched the engine come hurtling by, steam hissing and drive rods flying, high wheels whirling, open fire door blazing, a thunderous black dragon shiny with grease and speed. It was hard to believe that the fellow who drove this eight-wheeled lightning was a mere man. The engineer would lean from the cab window, casual as you please, one hand on the throttle, his eyes fixed on a spot about ten miles down the road.

When he got older and bolder, Casey would stand close beside the track and jump up and down like an electrified frog and wave his cap to draw the engineer's attention, and then pump his arm to show he wanted to hear the whistle. Now and again one of the drivers would actually notice him, flash a smile, and give a blast of steam. The sound lifted Casey up on his tiptoes and shook him silly. At times like that, he pitied the saints in heaven for having died before the coming of railroads.

"What's wrong with driving a plow up and down the furrows like your father?" Casey's mother wanted to know. "Why do you want to go tearing through the countryside behind a filthy, noisy engine?" She was a Grade A mother on most subjects, but she was blind and stubborn when it came to locomotives. "They stink," she declared. "Their racket dries up the cows and rattles down the plates in my cupboard. Their smoke leaves a skim of soot on the table and a black ring on my collar. Why is everybody in such a hurry and where are they going and what are they going to do when they get there?"

"Ma," Casey sighed, "You just don't understand."

"Indeed I don't," she said.

Casey's father did understand, because over the years he had grown tired of driving a plow up and down furrows. The awful thing about a furrow was, when you got to the far end of it you had to turn around and come back. Railroad tracks, now, they kept on going and going. Following them, you might see a new sight every day of your life. Casey's father had ears of his own. He listened to the trains roar past and felt the pull of distant places. There was a good deal more to see in the world than the back end of a horse, he figured. But he also figured he was too old and set in his ways for learning a new line of work. So he plowed and planted, manured and harvested, year after year, keeping his own restlessness a secret. But whenever Casey spoke eagerly to him about engines and steam and riding the rails, he understood every word and every silence.

When Casey finished with school at sixteen and begged leave to go take a job as a telegraph boy at the Columbus station, his mother was dead set against it. "You'll do nothing of the sort. You'll stay right here and help with the farming."

But his father said, "Go on ahead, if it's what you've a mind to do. Only promise me, if you ever get to driving one of them engines, you'll take me along on a trip sometime."

"Oh, you two are a pair," Casey's mother complained. "One of you gets an itch and both of you scratch. Railroads! I wish they were all at the bottom of the sea."

So Casey went up to Columbus and lived in a boarding-house. At the station he took down telegraph messages and passed word along to the signalmen. Trains stopped and started according to the messages he delivered; but it was not the same as holding the brake lever or throttle in your own hand. He went to work early and stayed on late, so he could hang around and listen to the off-duty railroaders talk. It was the richest kind of music, this talk about jerkwater towns and whistle stops and big cities, steep grades, milk runs, fast freights, wrecks and close shaves, deadheads, highballs, hobos riding on the bumpers, sweethearts waving hankies from second-story windows, pounds of steam and shades of smoke. Just the names of far-flung lines were enough to raise goose bumps: Erie-Lackawanna, Nickel Plate, Norfolk and Western, Southern Pacific, Illinois Central, Tug River and Kentucky, Santa Fe. Casey would rather sit in the corner and listen to such talk than eat biscuits and honey.

Not that he went hungry. At the boardinghouse he ate whatever the landlady put in front of him, and kept on eating until she got tired of carrying food in from the kitchen. By the age of nineteen he had stretched up to six feet and four inches, with brawn to match, big enough to get him out of the telegraph shack and onto the trains as a fireman shoveling coal. Now he was close to glory, working right next to the cab and watching every move the engineer made. Standing at the door of that furnace, Casey got a sense of what turkeys go through on Thanksgiving. But he put up with heat and coal dust in his throat and an ache in his back to stay there in the driver's shadow. All the engineers wanted Casey to stoke for them. He could get steam up quicker than any other man on the road, and he never slacked. No matter how hard you ran your hog, you could not burn coal faster than Casey could shovel.

Now and again, on a lazy downstretch where nothing could go wrong, the engineers let him take over the controls. It wasn't long before they were letting him climb hills and round curves, and pretty soon he was jockeying engines in the roundhouses and switching empty cars in the Memphis yards. Then by and by he was given his own engine, an old six-wheeler, to haul freight on the Illinois Central lines in Mississippi. And don't you know he puffed up with pride, sitting there on the driver's stool where every boy along the tracks could gawk at him! As soon as he got the chance, Casey meant to fetch his father for a ride.

He squeezed every grunt of speed out of that old hog. The stationmasters clucked their tongues when they wrote down the times that Casey made. If he could roll a burnt-out six-wheeler that fast, what would he do with a fresh eight-wheeler? They soon got a chance to find out just what he could do, for

Casey was sent to Chicago to fetch a brand-new hog, number 638, the biggest locomotive ever put on rails. With nothing to haul but a tender and caboose, Casey ran 638 down over the Illinois prairie so hard the fireman thought it would lift right off the tracks and fly. They stopped only for water and coal, and once, in Kentucky, to pick up Casey's father.

Above the engine's roar, Casey shouted, "Don't this beat a horse and buggy?"

On the far side of the cab his father was holding on for dear life and peeping out with startled eyes at the rushing countryside. "It does, if you live to tell about it!"

Casey laughed. "This ain't half fast. I'm still babying her. Wait until I get her broke in!" Then he yelled at the fireman to pour on more coal.

At Water Valley, down in Mississippi, they hitched on a string of freight cars for hauling to Canton. In the roundhouse when Casey finished his run, the mechanics and engine wipers and switchmen walked round and round that gleaming black locomotive, whistling in amazement. She looked like she was going thirty miles an hour when she was sitting still. Casey had to help his father down from the cab, the old man's legs were so shaky.

Next day they rode back to Water Valley, then returned the following day to Canton, then to Water Valley, to Canton, Water Valley, Canton, round and round for a week before Casey got Sunday off. By then his father was beginning to think this driving locomotives was an awful lot like driving plow horses up and down a furrow, only faster. You still had to turn around when you got to the other end and come right on back across the same ground, over and over again. Still, the speed was enough to stir up your blood. So he stayed on for a second week to ride with Casey between Water Valley and Canton, Canton and Water Valley. Before that week was out, he got used to the rush, the roar, the wind whistling past his ear. He got tired of breathing coal smoke. He could shut his eyes and recite the names of the small towns they kept passing through—Coffeeville, Grenada, Duck Hill, Winona, Durant, Pickens, Way—dusty crossroads that didn't look all that different from the two-bit burg in Kentucky where his wife was probably tapping her foot for him to come home.

At the end of that second week, Casey's father climbed off in Water Valley and said thanks for the ride but he had to be getting back to Ma.

Casey held onto his arm. "You don't reckon she'd like to come and have a ride, do you?"

The old man didn't have to think long. "Not hardly."

"Tell me how you liked it."

"Well, if a man has to run back and forth in a rut no matter what he works at, he might as well do it in style. And railroading's got a heap more style than farming does."

Casey took that as praise. In his opinion, the chief reason God had given us two legs instead of four was so that in the fullness of time we would get tired of walking and invent trains for getting around. He never could get enough of driving. The minute he stepped down from his engine at the end of a run, he slipped into a dark melancholy.

To cure his loneliness he studied the women who waved hankies at him from second-story windows along the track, picked out the prettiest one, and married her. She might have become lonely in turn, since Casey was all the time on the road, but before you knew it there were three little boys to look after. The boys wore Casey's old striped caps and lined up chairs beside the kitchen table to play train. Every time Casey drove by the house, day or night, he blew his whistle, and the boys hooted back at him. Mrs. Jones wore cotton in her ears.

Everybody within earshot of the Illinois Central road knew Casey's whistle. It was six notes long, and sounded like a cross between a calliope and a coyote. Sinners repented when they heard that moansome wail. It made children roll over on their pillows and dream about racing between stars. It made sweethearts whisper promises. There were even farm wives who swore that the sound of Casey's whistle made churned milk clabber sooner and chickens hurry up their eggs.

The owners of the Illinois Central did not care much about the speed of chickens, but they cared a great deal about the speed of trains, and they soon learned that nobody moved freight faster than Casey Jones. They put him and number 638 on the Cannonball Express, running south out of Memphis to Canton, and gave him the best fireman on the road, a cocoa-skinned man by the name of Sim Webb.

Soon the two of them got to be like brothers, the one always knowing what was in the other's head, they drove so many thousand miles together. Every few months, Casey and Sim set a new record for speed. Other engineers tried to match it, but nobody had the nerve. Even without Casey's whistle, folks could tell by the moan of the engine when the Cannonball was booming past.

Then one night it was pouring down to rain, the tracks

were as slick as a creekbed, and Casey finished his run into Memphis seventeen minutes late. He hated like the devil to come in behind schedule. He was grouching about this to Sim when the stationmaster came up to say the southbound engineer had called in sick, and would Casey mind staying over and taking the run back down to Canton.

Casey was bushed. But he answered, "Sure I'll drive, and by God I'll make up my lost time. You coming, Sim?"

"What you say, am I coming? If you driving, I'm firing."

They had to wait over an hour for the mail to arrive from Chicago. When they pulled out of Memphis it was near midnight and they were ninety minutes behind schedule. It was raining hard enough for catfish to grow in the fields.

"Let's get the old girl up on her toes and make her dance," Casey yelled at Sim.

Sim shouted back, "She gonna dance, all right, Mr. Casey! She gonna high-step right down the track!"

Casey drove with one hand on the whistle and one on the throttle. He blew and blew his six-note call, warning everyone to clear the road, the Cannonball was coming through, and he didn't plan to slow down for anything. The rain tore the light from his headlamp into shreds. He couldn't see more than a train's length ahead. All he could do was pray for open track. Downhill he ran at a hundred miles an hour, kept it near seventy through jerkwater towns, took curves at fifty. He pulled and pulled on that whistle cord. Dizzy-tired and giddy with speed, he hollered into the wind, "Look out the road, here we come!"

Sim shoveled as hard as he could go.

All along the route, hearing thunder roll by, people turned in bed and thought, Casey Jones.

By Grenada they had made up half their time. By Goodman they had caught up all but fifteen minutes. Casey kept looking at his watch, checking the steam gauge, squinting down the track. "If we don't explode first," he shouted, "we'll pass Way on time and coast on in to Canton!"

Sim didn't have breath to answer.

Swinging at double speed through the S-curve just north of Vaughn, Casey saw a red light up ahead on the siding. Or was it on the siding? It had to be. He stared into the rain, his heart going cold, wind and water on his face, knowing suddenly it was a lit-up caboose with its tail across the main tracks. Great merciful God, on time and no time and my time. In the few seconds he had left he grabbed the air-brake lever and cried, "Jump, Sim, jump!"

Sim jumped without waiting to ask why, hit the gravel, rolled safe into the bushes.

Casey hung all his weight on the brake lever and the whistle cord as the red light rushed toward him, huge, huge as the door of a furnace, and the caboose a pine box on wheels, and his ears filled with the howl of steam and steel.

The Devil and the Farmer's Wife

[TRADITIONAL]

Well, there was an old man lived up on the hill,
If he ain't moved away he's a-living there still.

> *Singing, hi, diddle-i, diddle-i fie!*
> *Diddle-i, diddle-i, day!*

The Devil came up to the farmer one day,
Says, "One of your family I'm a-going to take away."

"Well, please don't take my eldest son,
There's work on the farm that's gotta be done.

"But you can take my nagging wife,
By golly, she is the curse of my life."

So the Devil threw the old lady up over his back,
And went off to Hell with a clickety-clack.

Got her down to the fork of the road,
Says, "Old lady, you're one devil of a load!"

When he got her down to the gates of Hell,
Says, "Stoke up the fire, boys, we'll roast her well."

Come along a little devil with a ball and a chain,
She upped with her slipper foot and knocked out his brains.

Two little devils come a-peeking round the door,
She upped with her slipper, killed ninety-nine more.

Ten little devils just a-climbing up the wall,
Saying, "Take her back, Daddy, she'll murder us all!"

Well the farmer got up and he looked out a crack
Says, "Oh, my God, he's a-bringing her back!"

The farmer crawled up under his bed,
She yanked him out by the hair of his head.

Devil says, "Here's your wife, and I hope she's well,
If I'd a-kept her any longer she'd a-ruined Hell!

"Well, I've been a devil most all of my life,
But I never been in Hell till I met with your wife."

I guess this proves that women are better than men,
They can go down to Hell and come back again.

One time the Devil was dawdling along a road in Illinois, looking for trouble, when he got hungry. He took a handful of rock candy out of his pocket, threw it in his mouth, chewed it with his great pointy teeth, but still he was hungry. He knocked down seven crows with his snaky tail, gobbled them up, but the feathers tickled the inside of his stomach and only made him hungrier. He came to an orchard of early apples, cooked them nice and brown with a single huff of his breath, ate the whole orchard. Same thing! Hungry as the ocean waiting for the moon to come up. What he needed was a fresh soul, the meaner the better.

About that time he heard grunts and groans and a loud scolding voice coming from the next hill. He could pretty much count on finding sinners wherever he found people, so he walked on up that hill and came to a tumbledown house, and behind the house there was a tottery barn, and behind the barn there was a stony field. A man and a gawky boy were harnessed to a plow, tugging until their eyes bulged. A little bit of a girl was stumbling along behind the plow, trying to keep it straight in the furrow. A woman sat on a stool in the shade, fanning herself with a starched bonnet, sipping cider, and when the Devil arrived she was yelling, "Daughter, hold that plow square! I don't want to look out here when that corn comes up and see crooked rows. Son, don't you tear those britches, or you'll mend them yourself! Husband, put your back into it! Do you think that dirt's going to break open with you barely scratching at it?" The daughter whined, the son wailed, and the husband wheezed.

The Devil rubbed his hands. Here was good eating for sure. Hard luck meant hard feelings, and nothing tasted better to the Devil than angry folks. To get everybody's attention he called down some lightning and thumped his tail on the ground. Well, you know they looked at him pretty quick. The man and the boy stopped dead still, leaning into the harness, and the girl grabbed on to the plow handle for dear life. Their faces turned milky and their teeth started clacking. The woman on the stool quit yelling in the middle of a sentence, but she didn't shake and she didn't tremble. She just gave the Devil a scowl that would have raised blisters on a pig.

The Devil slouched up to the man and said, "Look here, farmer, I've come to take away somebody in your family. Which one's it going to be? How about that little bit of a girl?"

The farmer took a minute to find his tongue. Then he begged, "O mercy no, you can't have my daughter. Who'd milk the cows? Who'd feed the chickens? Who'd cook supper? Who'd sit beside the fire and brush her yellow hair?"

"Then how about this gawky boy?"

"O mercy no. The mule's sick. If you took my son, who'd help me pull the plow? Who'd gather walnuts? Who'd make up songs in the barn?"

"Then how about this ornery wife of yours?" said the Devil.

The farmer's face cracked open with a smile. "You're welcome to her."

The farmer's wife jumped up off her stool, clapped the bonnet on her head, and yelled, "William Jay, just what do you think you're up to, giving me away like a sack of potatoes? I'll snatch you bald! I'll stretch your ugly ears until you can tie them in a bow!"

"Now, Martha," said the farmer, "who am I to argue with the Devil?"

"Nobody, that's who! You're about as brave as a two-legged turtle! Why, you wouldn't talk back to a frog if it ate your breakfast!" She flung her stool at the farmer, but he ducked and the stool hit the Devil right smack between the horns. Clonk! Broke into about a thousand match sticks and raised a lump.

If the Devil hadn't been so hungry, he might have known right then and there to go looking for a tamer soul. But he wouldn't listen to anything except his belly, and his belly wanted food *now*.

"Come on, old lady," the Devil told the farmer's wife. He

stuffed her in his sack, threw her over his shoulder, and took off carrying her down the road.

The farmer and his boy and girl stood in the field, watching. Not a one of them frowned.

Well, just because she was stuffed in a sack, that didn't stop Martha from squirming and jostling, hollering and scolding. It was all the Devil could do to stay on the road, she raised so much Cain.

"Old lady," he panted, "I've hauled four wrestlers in this bag at one time, and nine horse-traders along with their horses, and a whole congregation of snake-swallowers, but I never carried any load that gave me as much trouble as you do!"

"You just let me out of here and I'll teach you what trouble is! I'll jerk a knot in your neck, you fork-tongued, fork-toed, fork-tailed cousin to a wart hog! You scaly old stink-pot!"

The Devil ran faster, staggering from side to side, down the road to Hell. Some of his little devils were playing catch with a ball of fire outside the gates when he came puffing along. "Run fetch a chain," he said, "and help me tie up our supper."

In about half a minute, here they came dragging a chain, clankety-clank. But when the Devil opened the sack to grab the woman, she punched him in the nose so hard his eyes rolled up. Out she jumped, seized hold of that chain, slung little devils in the air and started whomping them as fast as they landed.

"Help, Daddy, help!" they squealed. "She's going to mash us into butter!"

When the Devil got his eyes straightened out and saw what was what, he wrapped his tail around that woman and squeezed. He wouldn't be able to keep a hold on her for long, the way she was thrashing, so he hollered, "Run poke up the fire, boys! We'll roast her and toast her and eat her quick!"

The woman bucked and shouted, still wrapped in the Devil's tail. "Think again, you old lizard-faced skunkbait! There isn't a man or devil born who could roast me if I wasn't ready to be roasted."

Well, they threw on the wood and got that fire roaring. But before the Devil could drag her to the flames she bit down on his tail and just about chomped it in two. He yelped and let her go and stuck his tail in his mouth to lick it. She kicked him in both knees, smacked him on the bump the stool had raised between his horns, and twisted his hairy goat's ears. He went hopping from hoof to hoof, yowling. The little devils came charging in to help, but the farmer's wife took off her slipper and swatted them left and right, like squishy flies, and before you knew it they had all scampered up the walls and across the ceiling, and they hung up there by their claws, pleading, "Take her back, Daddy! Take her on back before she ruins Hell!"

Hungry or not, the Devil knew when he'd bitten off more than he could chew. It was all he could do to wrestle that woman back into his bag. Then off he went as fast as he could hobble, out through the gates of Hell and up the road into Illinois.

The farmer was just rolling out of bed next morning when he heard the two of them coming along the drive, the woman scolding and the Devil grunting.

"O my God," the farmer said, peering out through a crack in the wall, "he's bringing her back!" He scuttled under the bed and lay there breathing dust.

The Devil opened the front door and shouted, "Here you go, farmer, and you're welcome to her! I've been down below since a little while after the Creation, but I never knew what Hell was until I met your wife!" With that he dumped her from the sack onto the cabin floor. Then he leapt back out the door, but not before she had time to stomp on his tail. Down the road the Devil went, lickety-split, holding his tail and limping.

"Will you look at the mess they make as soon as I turn my back!" Martha said, staring around at the cabin. "William Jay! Where are you hiding your lazy bones?" Bending down, she spied him under the bed and jerked him out by his top-knot. "There you are! Tell me now, what are yesterday's dishes still doing in the pan? Why's that rug all rumpled? How is it there's no fire laid and it's breakfast time? Why are the cows mooing? What's my teapot doing there on the corner of the table where the first clumsy ox that goes by is sure to knock it off? How'd your beard get so full of dust? You look like a mop that needs shaking."

The son and daughter, who had been sleeping in the loft, woke up to all the screeching. The girl whispered, "Sounds like Mammy's home."

"I told you the Devil would be sorry," said the boy.

"And as for you two," Martha shouted up the ladder into the loft, "quit your lollygagging and get down here and start your chores! If there isn't a fire going and bacon frying inside of five minutes, I'll tan the daylights out of both of you!"

Well, the fur flew around that cabin for a week or so. Neighbors put up their shutters and stuffed beeswax into their ears, Martha hollered so loud. Then she calmed down a bit, settled into a comfortable sort of high temper, and stayed mad for years and years, until her children were grown and moved away and her husband was worried into his grave.

Mean as she was, that didn't keep Martha from wearing out like everybody else. One day she was obliged to die. First she traipsed on up to Heaven, since that was the choicer place. St. Peter sat behind the gates, combing his beard. He looked out through the bars and his eyes swelled wide open.

"Why, Martha," he said, "what would you be looking for?"

"What do you think?" she snapped. "I want in, you long-jawed lummox!"

St. Peter left the comb stuck in his beard and took a step back from the gates. "Well now, I'm afraid I can't let you in."

"Tell me why not, and be quick about it!"

"Just look here at your record." From a safe distance behind the bars, St. Peter showed her the Great Book opened to her name. "You see here where the page for good deeds hasn't got but two or three lines filled in, and here the page for wickedness is written top to bottom, crossways, along the margins, and there's words hanging over the edge?"

"Who keeps that blamed book? Let me have a few words with him!" Martha gave the gates a good hard rattle. A flock of angels came flying up to protect St. Peter, took one look at her, and flew back into the clouds.

"I keep it," St. Peter answered, "but I just remembered some place I've got to go." And away he went.

"You can have your old Heaven!" Martha yelled after him. "It looks too quiet to suit me!"

So she traipsed on down to Hell. The little devils were out playing catch with fireballs again when they saw her coming. They ran inside, called their daddy, and hid behind his great thick legs, shivering. The Devil squinted out at Martha. Just looking at her roused up aches all over his body. "You get lost or something?" he said.

"No, I'm not lost, you goat-nosed blowhard," she said. "I've come to stay. Open up and let me in!"

"Not on your life!" said the Devil.

Martha stamped her foot so hard the Devil's long fangs shook in his jaw. "Well, if they won't have me up above, and you won't have me down below, where in tarnation am I going to go?"

"Tell you what," said the Devil, throwing a red-hot coal out through the bars and heaving a pair of tongs after it, "take that fire and go somewhere a long way off and start your own Hell."

What could she do but grab the tongs and pick up the fire and wander off? That was a long while back. But if you go in the woods at night and look until you find the right place, you can still see her coal glowing white on the stump of an old dead tree. Folks who don't know any better will call that foxfire. But you and I know the truth, now, don't we?

Frankie and Johnny

[TRADITIONAL]

Frankie and Johnny were lovers,
O lordy how they could love,
Swore to be true to each other,
True as the stars above.
    He was her man, but he done her wrong.

Little Frankie was a good gal,
As everybody knows,
She did all the work around the house,
And pressed her Johnny's clothes.
    He was her man, but he done her wrong.

Johny was a yeller man,
With coal black, curly hair.
Everyone up in St. Louis
Thought he was a millionaire.
    He was her man, but he done her wrong.

Frankie and Johnny went walking,
Johnny in his brand-new suit.
"O good Lawd," says Frankie,
"Don't my Johnny look cute?"
    He was her man, but he done her wrong.

Frankie went down to the barroom,
Called for a bottle of beer,
Says, "Looky here, Mr. Bartender,
Has my lovingest man been here?
    He is my man, but he's doing me wrong."

"I will not tell you no story,
I'll not tell you no lie.
Johnny left here about an hour ago,
With a gal named Nelly Bly.
    He is your man, and he's doing you wrong."

Little Frankie went down Broadway,
With her pistol in her hand,
Says, "Stand aside you chorus gals,
I'm a-looking for my man.
    He is my man, but he's doing me wrong."

Johnny saw Frankie a-coming,
Down the back stairs he did scoot.
Frankie had the little gun out,
Let him have it, rooty-toot-toot.
    He was her man, but she shot him down.

The first time she shot him, he staggered,
The next time she shot him, he fell,
The last time she shot, O Lawdy,
There was a new man's face in Hell.
    She shot her man, for doing her wrong.

"Turn me over doctor,
Turn me over slow,
I got a bullet in my left-hand side,
Great God it's hurting me so.
    I was her man, but I done her wrong."

Bring on your rubber-tired buggy,
Bring on your rubber-tired hack,
They're taking Johnny to the graveyard,
And they won't bring a bit of him back.
He was her man, but he done her wrong.

It was not murder in the first degree,
It was not murder in the third.
A woman simply dropped her man
Like a hunter drops his bird.
She shot him down for doing her wrong.

Walked on down Broadway,
As far as I could see,
All I could hear was a two-string bow,
Playing "Nearer, My God, to Thee."
He was her man, and he done her wrong.

A woman's life is a mighty long crooked row to hoe, the way Frankie looked at it. She grew up without a daddy and with only about one-eighth of a mammy, there were so many other children in the house, and never quite enough food to fill every belly, and freezing in winter when the coal gave out, and all the men who passed through the door meaner than junkyard dogs. Frankie watched her mammy wear out from work and mothering, like a dress scrubbed too many times in lye. When Frankie turned thirteen she couldn't run off the way her brothers did, she had to stay home and nurse the little ones, and also to nurse Mammy, who was frazzled down to wrinkles and bones. Before Mammy died, Frankie took a study of her plowed-over face and promised herself, I ain't ever going to let that happen to me.

With her mammy dead and no men in sight and four mouths still at home chirping for food like blackbirds in a nest, Frankie had to find paying work. And what did she know how to do but cook and clean and look after small fry? You could do all that under your own roof for a lifetime, and nobody would ever pay you a nickel; but find a white lady with too much money on her hands, and she would pay you silver dollars to run her house. Frankie found a white lady in St. Louis. As mistresses go, this one took the prize for kindness. She bought Frankie a flouncy dress and a starched apron, let her carry home kitchen scraps, gave her hand-me-down clothes. If one of Frankie's brothers or sisters fell sick, the mistress let her bring the ailing child along to work. Since the white lady's own children were grown, she enjoyed coming by to pinch the cheeks of Frankie's little ones. So long as you have to fetch and do for other folks, Frankie reckoned, you might as well fetch and do for somebody with a heart instead of a lump of ice.

Frankie got up before the sun to fix a day's food for her own house, then went to the white folks' place to scrub and cook until dark, then came back home and washed up and put away and mended. Falling into bed at last was sweeter than corn syrup. She saved her money in a crock. Once a month she counted it, and wrote the sum on a piece of butcher paper. That trail of numbers kept her going from year to year. When she got enough saved she was going to buy a café, and then she would cook her own kind of food for people with her own dark skin, be her own boss, close the doors when she felt like a holiday, never again say yes ma'am or no ma'am, never smile except when she felt like smiling.

Between looking after two houses and raising up her little brothers and sisters, Frankie had no lazy time for walking out with boys. She hardly even saw a pair of britches from one week to the next. Now and again some of her mammy's mean old boyfriends came prancing by and thumped on the door, but Frankie never would let them in. "You keep coming round," she would yell out the window, "and next time I'll pour the dishwater on you and maybe leave in the frying pan for weight."

The only place Frankie was sure to see men was at the kitchen door of the white folks' house, but the only ones her own color were the ashman, the iceman, and the milkman, and every living soul of them was married.

Then one morning the bell over the front door rang. Mighty early for visitors, Frankie thought, as she opened up. And there on the porch stood a delivery boy as shiny brown as a chestnut, holding a bunch of red carnations all wrapped in tissue paper. He looked stiff and full of business until he caught sight of her, and then he loosened up.

He swept off his cap. "Morning, princess. Where'd you park your carriage?"

"It's in the garage with a broke wheel," Frankie shot back. "Now tell me what about these flowers and let me get to work."

The delivery boy kept giving her the glad eye. Frankie could see by the way he held himself, all spruced up like a peacock, that every female who'd ever crossed his tracks had called him handsome. "The Master sends these to the Missus on her birthday," he said, handing Frankie the carnations. "And now, princess, since your carriage is broke, how about if I walk you home tonight?"

"I know the way myself," said Frankie, shutting the door.

That was in the fall. At Christmas time he rang the bell again to deliver a bouquet of roses. Frankie let him woof at her for a few minutes before taking the flowers.

"Missus get the roses, and you get me," he said.

Frankie had to admit he looked good enough to put in a stocking over the fireplace. But she never let on. All she said was, "You got enough brass in you to make a kettle out of."

"Purest brass in St. Louis. And what do you call yourself, heart-breaker?"

"I don't give out my name to strangers."

"I do, but only to pretty gals. Any time you want me to come running, just holler Johnny."

At Easter he brought an armful of lilies. "These are for the Missus," he announced, "but I'd rather give them to you, heart-string." She let him sweet-talk for half an hour.

That night when she stepped outside for the walk back home, Johnny sidled up to her carrying a single pale lily. It caught all the light in the sky and shimmered like a moon-moth.

"I bet that's one of the Missus's," she scolded.

"She got more than she can count," said Johnny, "and anyway you be the true princess."

He knew how to walk so as to stretch out the distance. He

could talk bark off a tree, he was that slick with his tongue. When they got to her place, Johnny crawled under the table and played bear-in-a-cage with the little ones while Frankie did up the dishes. Every night after that for a month he met her at the back door with a leftover flower and walked her home, woofing sweetly all the way. And then just naturally he brought his pillow to her place and moved in.

For a while things were as good as things ever get. Johnny kept running deliveries, Frankie kept running the white lady's house; nights and Sundays they had to themselves. The little ones just ate Johnny up, the way he teased them and swaddled them in stories. Frankie didn't mind doing all the cooking and cleaning and ironing, so long as Johnny minded the children and filled the kitchen with his honeysome voice.

With both of them earning pay, she figured the crock would fill up in no time, and they could buy a café together. Johnny swore there wasn't a thing on earth he'd rather do than own a café. "Can't you just see me sitting at the back table in a bow tie and curled mustache?" But somehow he never had any money left at the weekend. "I got expenses, you know. I got appearances to keep up."

Frankie kept stashing away her dimes and dollars, kept adding the figures on her piece of butcher paper.

One night Johnny came to meet her after work and he didn't carry a flower and didn't have on his delivery uniform. He was sucking on a peppermint, but he still smelled of whiskey.

"You got the boot," Frankie said, a blue sadness coming over her.

"The boss and me had a brouhaw, that's true. Don't you worry, heart-throb. I'll find me a new job tomorrow."

Days went by, and no job. Johnny quit walking her home. He stumbled in early or late, shifty as a tomcat, smelling of tobacco and booze.

"Who you hanging around with when you ain't working?" Frankie demanded.

Johnny put on a choirboy's innocent face. "Just because I'm out of a job, why you go accusing me? Rest your mind, Queen-of-Egypt. I'm your number one man and your number two and three. I'm as true to you as the stars above."

Next time Frankie took down her crock she found it short three dollars, and in place of the money there was an IOU from Johnny. She decided not to raise sand about it this one time. A man has his pride. But a few nights later she found an IOU for two-fifty, and then she lit into him. "What you doing stealing my café money?"

"I ain't stealing it," said Johnny, cool as you please. "I'm borrowing it."

"What for?"

He slid his eyes away from her. "I got expenses."

"Stand on your hind legs and get a job, and you can pay your own expenses."

"Now, babe," he said, putting the syrup into his voice, "how am I going to land a job with nothing but these rags to wear?"

"They don't hire your clothes," said Frankie.

"They do in the line of work I'm aiming at."

"Which is what?"

"Door-to-door salesman."

With his looks and his tongue, he ought to be able to sell ice to Eskimos, she figured. Anyway, he could still sell her any pretty yarn he made up. She dug forty dollars out of her crock and gave it to him. That night he met her after work dressed up in new patent leather shoes and a gleaming blue suit and a black fedora hat with the brim curled. If the angel Gabriel had come down from Heaven and put on clothes, he couldn't have looked any better than Johnny.

"I done already got me a job selling ointments and remedies," he said.

Frankie noticed the pearl handle of a revolver sticking out of his pocket. "What's that cannon for?"

He laughed. "That's for persuading the folks who don't go for my sales pitch."

For a while things were like silk between them. At night Johnny met Frankie at the door of the white lady's house, and told about all the remedies he had sold that day. He always smelled a little ripe, walked a little tipsy. But Frankie didn't rag him about drinking so long as he was working.

The only trouble was, he never brought a penny home. Every time she looked in her crock, there was money gone, without even an IOU. Frankie didn't like the smell of things. So one day she begged the white lady to let her off at noon for a funeral, and went home, and there was Johnny, dead asleep in bed, and the little ones all next door at a neighbor's. Frankie took and hid the pistol in one of her old shoes, to keep him from getting up to mischief. Then she backed out of the house and stood in a doorway across the street, waiting. Midway in the afternoon, out stepped Johnny in his dazzling blue suit. She followed him down the street to a smoky tavern, and watched him through the window as he bought drinks and played cards. Before quitting time she went on back to the white lady's house, just to see what Johnny would say when he picked her up.

"I done nearly walked my pins off today, selling ointments," he told her that evening.

"Humph! Only wear and tear you got is in your elbow, lifting bottles and flipping cards," she fired back.

"What you saying, girl?"

"I'm saying I seen how you pass your days, squandering my café money."

"Now, dumpling . . ."

"Don't you dumpling me! You got more lies in you than the Missouri railroad's got crossties."

Johnny stomped on away from her, reached home first, cleaned out the crock and left a note saying, "IOU One Café."

Frankie straightened the house, emptied the sink, and sang the little ones to sleep. Then she took off looking for Johnny. When she didn't find him at the tavern, she asked the bartender, "Have you seen my man?"

"Why, sure. Johnny's been by."

"Where'd he go?" Frankie slapped the bar. "And don't tell me no lies! I'm fed up with lies."

The bartender wrinkled his forehead. "He took off from here for the Hotel Ritz."

"And I bet he wasn't alone."

"Naw, ma'am. He had Miss Alice Fry on his arm."

Frankie caught a look at herself in the mirror over the bar.

What she saw was her mother's pinched and furrowed face. "Oh, no, it ain't going to happen to me!" she cried, whirling around. "I won't stand for it!" She ran home, got the pearl-handled pistol and tucked it under her apron, then hurried to the Ritz Hotel.

Johnny was dancing with a waxy-haired gal in the ballroom when he spied Frankie charging at him. He let loose of that gal and turned on his nine-dollar grin. "Now listen to me, heart-string, this ain't how it looks!"

"You call this being true as the stars above?"

"I got explanations!"

"What you got is trouble! I done put up with all I'm going to put up with!" Frankie drew the pistol from beneath her apron.

The ballroom cleared in a hurry. Johnny backed away, hands fluttering, the grin turning hard like an overcooked egg. "Now, princess," he murmured, "listen at me just a minute . . ."

To shut him up, Frankie lifted the pistol and fired at the wall beside him. At least she was aiming at the wall, but the bullet caught Johnny in the chest and spun him around and threw him on the floor, and there he lay in his shimmery blue suit and shiny black shoes while she bent over him shrieking.

Too long, too long it took for the doctor to come. Frankie offered to pay him any price if only he would save Johnny. But her man was beyond medicine.

"Roll me over slow, babe," Johnny whispered. "Roll me on my right side, for the left one hurts me so."

Frankie had her fingers on his pretty face when he died.

They let her out of jail for the funeral. The only music was a two-string band on the corner playing, "Nearer, My God, to Thee." Frankie walked behind the rubber-tired hearse all the way to the cemetery, tearing up lilies and throwing them on the street.

The Frozen Logger

[BY JAMES STEVENS]

As I sat down one evening
Within a small café,
A forty-year-old waitress,
To me these words did say:

"I see you are a logger,
And not a common bum,
For no one but a logger
Stirs his coffee with his thumb.

"My lover was a logger,
There's none like him today;
If you poured whiskey on it,
He'd eat a bale of hay.

"He never shaved the whiskers
From off his horny hide,
But he drove them in with a hammer
And bit them off inside.

"My lover came to see me
On one freezing day,
He held me in a fond embrace
That broke three vertebrae.

"He kissed me when we parted
So hard he broke my jaw.
I could not speak to tell him
He'd forgot his mackinaw.

"I saw my logger lover
Sauntering through the snow,
A-going gaily homeward
At forty-eight below.

"The weather tried to freeze him,
It tried its level best.
At one hundred degrees below zero
He buttoned up his vest.

"It froze clean through to China,
It froze to the stars above,
At one thousand degrees below zero
It froze my logger love.

"They tried in vain to thaw him,
And if you'll believe me, sir,
They made him into ax blades
To chop the Douglas fir.

"And so I lost my lover,
And to this café I come,
And here I wait till someone
Stirs his coffee with his thumb."

*O*ne February afternoon some kids were skating on Thief River, way up in the north woods of Minnesota. And was it cold? Inside of five minutes they stopped getting messages from their fingers and toes. They had to keep looking down at their skates to make sure there were still feet on the ends of their legs. It was so cold their shouts froze in the air and they could read what everybody was saying from the curlicues of breath. Now and again they stood beside a fire on the river bank and flapped their arms, but all that did was boil steam from their scarves and fill their noses with the smell of toasted wool. Before long they were aching for hot chocolate. So they skated on numb legs downstream to Thief River Falls, where they piled into Gertie's Café.

Big and sad-eyed, Gertie limped back and forth behind the counter like a bear with sore paws. Her white hair was piled in the shape of a beaver lodge, and the heap seemed large enough to hide an actual beaver. She had three pencils stuck into it at different angles. None of the kids knew how old she was, but she must have been way up there, because the skin of her face looked like the river ice when it starts to break up in the spring.

"I suppose you're going to want marshmallows in that cocoa," said Gertie.

Still slow of jaw from the cold, the kids nodded yes, yes, they'd love marshmallows.

"And I suppose you're going to want doughnuts to dunk in it," said Gertie.

The kids nodded.

"And spoons to stir it with?"

The kids blinked in puzzlement.

"You wouldn't be lifting your eyebrows at me," said Gertie, sloshing a mug of cocoa in front of each skater, "if you'd ever met a real lumberjack. That's how I always pick them out from ordinary men, you know, because an old-time logger stirs his coffee with his thumb."

The kids looked from their thumbs to their steaming mugs and back again, but chose not to experiment. They munched doughnuts and blew on the cocoa, waiting for a story. Gertie always served a story, no matter what you ordered to eat.

"Oh, good land, bring me back those old loggers!" She clattered an armful of dishes into the sink behind the counter and began scrubbing them as she talked. Watching her splash away, the kids understood why all the café dishes were chipped. "I can remember a time," said Gertie, "when half the men who came in here wore red shirts and green suspenders and never touched a fork or a spoon. I'd serve them stacks of blackberry pancakes and they'd shovel them in with bare hands. They picked the seeds out of their teeth with bowie knives. I had to empty my kitchen to fill them up. And when they were stuffed they'd put their caulked boots on the tables and comb lice out of their beards."

"Lice!" one of the girls whispered.

"They were a bit rough on the outside," Gertie conceded, "but underneath they were as gentle as lambs. Perfect lambs. You take Otto the Finn, for instance. Now there was a lovable man. Oh, he looked like something that had crawled out of a cave, all shaggy and mean. He was so big you would catch a cold from walking through his shadow. Most of one ear was missing, his nose bent in three directions, and his forehead was a regular road map of scars. But, saints above, he was a gorgeous man! When Otto gave you a hug, you stayed hugged for a week."

Gertie leaned back from the sink and fell silent, her eyes gone all daydreamy. The soapsuds made her brawny forearms look like the front legs of a polar bear.

The kids were beginning to thaw. One of them said, "You got any more marshmallows?"

Gertie looked up from the sink as if she had forgotten the children were there. "You bet," she said, drying her fists on her apron. She took the pot of cocoa and bag of marshmallows and refilled each mug. As she poured, she resumed her story. "Otto used to sit there, chewing, and watch me everywhere I went. 'Get your eyes full and fill your pockets,' I'd tell him, and laugh, you know, to show I didn't mind. He just stared. So one time I asked him, 'What do you find so all-fired interesting to look at?' And he said, in that rumbly Finnish voice of his, 'I been six months without seeing angels, so now when I got one nearby I give her a good look.' Ha! You see what a sweetheart he was underneath? There for a few years he came through every fall when he was heading north to the lumber camps, and again every spring when he was riding the logs down river to the sawmills."

"Like a migrating caribou," one of the boys observed.

"I guess you could say that." Gertie plunged her arms once again into the sudsy sink. "We never had what you'd call a romance. How could we? I had to stay here and run my café, and Otto had to go off to the woods. Half the time he talked to me in Finnish, but I could usually figure it out by reading that scarred-up face of his. Once when I had trouble understanding him, he sharpened his ax and shaved his beard with it so I could get a better look at his lips."

"What was he trying to say?" asked one of the kids.

"He wanted to know if we had bedbugs here in town like they had in the lumber shanty, and did folks in town have to wake up every morning at four with the cook banging a frying pan over our heads, and did we work all day in snow up to our knees until nine or ten at night, chopping by lantern light, and did we sleep fifteen or twenty of us side by side under one long blanket with our boots for pillows to keep them from freezing, and did our socks roast on the drying racks like rotten fish, and did we ache in every joint, and by and large what sort of life did we live here in town."

"I see why you had trouble understanding all that in Finnish," said a girl.

"Once I worked it out, it all boiled down to one question."

Several voices said, "What was that?"

"Otto was trying to figure out if he wanted to quit lumbering and marry me and live upstairs over my café."

"You mean he was *proposing?*" asked one of the boys.

"Oh, he didn't know it. He thought he was just passing the time with a girl in a café."

The kids slurped their cocoa, trying to imagine wrinkled, white-haired, sad-eyed Gertie young enough to be called a girl.

"That was in the fall," Gertie went on, her voice rising above the clatter of dishes, "and Otto went on north into the woods without putting the question directly. But I knew he'd

come back. And sure enough, one blizzardy day in January he came stomping through the door wearing two inches of snow. He gave me a hug that cracked my vertebrae and lifted me up off the floor and slung me around like a sack of potatoes. As a matter of fact, that's what he called me. 'Sweet potato,' he said, with me still two feet off the ground in his arms, 'I just figure something out, and I walk in from camp to find what you think.' Straightaway I told him, 'I think it's a great idea.' He put me down. He had a square face the size of a breadbox, and every scar and crease in it stretched into a grin. 'You *do?*' he said. 'Sure,' I told him. 'I been needing a man around here since my daddy died.' He let out a whoop and flung his cap at the ceiling. And I gave him a big fat kiss right on the lips."

The kids rocked on their stools, clapping for Gertie. "So you got married?" somebody said.

"That was the plan." Gertie's hands quit moving in the sink. She stared at the grease-speckled wall, and her voice seemed to come from a long way off. "Otto couldn't quit on his buddies in the middle of the season, so he was going back to camp until spring. Then he'd ride the logs down Thief River and stop here with me and never go away again. I fed him up while he was here, about a wheelbarrow's worth of grub. He got so hot between the food and the café and us talking about marriage that he took off six layers of clothes. But when he got dressed to go he only put five layers back on. He left his mackinaw hanging on the coat rack, and I never noticed it until too late, because the last thing he did was to give me a kiss that about dislocated my jaw, and while

I stood at the window watching him disappear into the blizzard I wasn't thinking about mackinaws or anything else at all except spring."

Gertie fell silent again. The kids nervously bumped their heels against the rungs of their stools, ran fingers around the rims of their mugs, glancing at one another to see what they were supposed to make of this story. At last somebody said, "And did he come back in the spring?"

"No, he didn't, the poor big ox. Tough as he was, he needed that mackinaw. It must have been umpty-dozen degrees below zero when he left here that night, and him out walking through a blizzard with only his vest on, and it getting colder by the minute. In the blackness and the air thick with snow and his heart all stirred up with love, he walked right past the camp. When they found him he was seven miles too far up Thief River."

"Found him?" said one of the kids.

"Frozen hard as an ax blade. They hauled him back here and he still wasn't all the way thawed out when we buried him."

The kids stared at the dregs of chocolate in their mugs. After a little while somebody said, "That wasn't how I thought it was going to come out at all. That's awful sad."

"Some stories are," said Gertie. She pulled the plug in the sink, and the water began draining with a gurgle. Dried on the apron, her forearms looked raw and red. "You galoots want any more refills?"

The kids all shook their heads, then ran home on tingly feet.

Jesse James

[TRADITIONAL]

It was on a Wednesday night, the moon was shining bright,
They robbed the Glendale train.
And the people they did say, for many miles away,
'Twas the outlaws Frank and Jesse James.

Jesse had a wife to mourn all her life,
The children they were brave.
But that dirty little coward shot Mister Howard
And laid Jesse James in his grave.

It was Robert Ford, the dirty little coward,
I wonder how he does feel,
For he ate of Jesse's bread and he slept in Jesse's bed,
Then he laid Jesse James in his grave.

It was his brother Frank that robbed the Gallatin bank,
And carried the money from the town.
It was in this very place that they had a little race,
For they shot Captain Sheets to the ground.

They went to the crossing not very far from there,
And there they did the same;
And the agent on his knees he delivered up the keys
To the outlaws Frank and Jesse James.

It was on a Saturday night, Jesse was at home,
Talking to his family brave,
When the thief and the coward, little Robert Ford,
Laid Jesse James in his grave.

How people held their breath when they heard of Jesse's death,
And wondered how he ever came to die.
It was one of the gang, dirty Robert Ford,
That shot Jesse James on the sly.

Jesse went to his rest with his hand on his breast.
The Devil will be upon his knee.
He was born one day in the county of Clay,
And came from a solitary race.

The more money he stole and the more guards he left shot-up and bleeding, the more Jesse James was troubled by a question: Am I a wicked man, or am I a saint? No matter where he traveled with his gang, in Missouri and the neighboring states, he could read in the newspapers strong opinions of his character. "Jesse James is a slinking, dirty-dealing, weasel-gutted desperado," one paper might declare, while the next one might say, "Jesse James is a modern-day Robin Hood, stealing from the rich and giving to the poor, a man with a heart as big as a washtub."

Sometimes Jesse's heart truly felt as big as a washtub, it swelled up with so much anger or pity. Once he was knocking over a bank in Kansas City with his brother Frank, just a little two-bit job, hardly worth the trouble, and everybody was nice and quiet with their hands in the air, when a young punk of a teller standing next to him spat a gob of tobacco juice that splashed onto Jesse's new boots. And—boom! Jesse filled up with a red-hot fury. By the time he could see straight, his gun was smoking and the teller was sprawled on the floor.

For months after that, every time he looked down and noticed the worm-shaped stains on his boots, he would get mad all over again. And wouldn't you know the teller was married, which meant another widow sat around hating Jesse's guts.

But Jesse could also think of a widow here and there who would kiss the ground he walked on. One time he and Frank and the gang were making a getaway after a job in New Madrid, riding hard, and they all got parched and hungry, so they stopped at a farmhouse to get something to eat. The six of them tramped into the kitchen, guns on their hips and spurs jingling. A scrawny woman—not much more than a girl, really, with a long, horsy face tied up in a green bandanna as if she had a toothache—was lifting a pan of biscuits out of the oven. She took one look at them and burst out crying.

"We won't harm a hair on your head," Jesse told her. "All we want is some food." She fed them, weeping all the while, until finally Jesse got a little burned up from listening to her. "I done told you we don't mean no harm. What do you keep on blubbering for?"

She tugged loose a corner of the green bandanna and used it to dab at her eyes. "I'm not scared," she said. "It's just that seeing you all there at the table with your sleeves rolled up and your jaws going makes me think of my dead husband."

Jesse swept off his hat and laid it over his chest like the lid on a pot. Already he could feel the pity beginning to simmer inside him. "How'd he die, ma'am?"

"The bull gored him," she said.

"How long ago?"

"A year ago tomorrow." As if her dams had burst she poured her grief over them—about her two children going barefoot to school, the barn roof leaking, the cows drying up, the mortgage overdue on the farm and a man coming from the bank to foreclose if she didn't find twelve hundred dollars by noon.

That brought Jesse's pity to the boil. He reached into the satchel containing the haul from that morning's stickup and counted out fifteen hundred dollars on the kitchen table. "You pay the bank man," he said, "and be sure you get a receipt from him, and use the extra for the barn and the kids' shoes."

The yellow-haired woman kissed him and thanked him and stood outside in the herb garden waving at him as he rode away. The gang waited in the bushes down the road a piece and watched the bank official ride past on his way to the farmhouse. Later on, when he rode by their hiding place again on his way back to town, they jumped him and stole the money all over. Jesse was still out three hundred dollars, but it was worth it to have a widow praying for him.

So there he was: some widows praising him and others cursing him. He could say the same for farmers. The gang went through horses pretty fast, between hard riding and gunshots from posses, so they had to steal fresh ones fairly often. Whenever he had the time and money, Jesse liked to pay for the horses he stole. He might leave three or four times what the horses were worth, stuck on a nail in the barn. But when the gang was short of cash, they swept through a horse lot, grabbed what they needed, and rode away. The farmers who found all those greenbacks nailed to their barn just shook their heads and smiled; the ones who didn't get paid shook their fists.

Sheriffs hated him, of course, and so did bankers and railroad bosses. But there were beggars in five states who blessed him for squeezing hundred dollar bills into their palms, and there were poor folks in a dozen towns eating food and wearing clothes bought with money Jesse had slipped under the doors of churches. He knew where it said in the Bible, "Thou shalt not steal," and, "Thou shalt not kill." But he refused to think of what he did as stealing; it was just moving riches from those who had a lot to those who had a little. The killing was harder to get around. But didn't a man have the right to protect himself? Wasn't that the first law of creation?

Sometimes he would tug the brim of his hat down low and drop by a tavern and steer the talk around to the subject of Jesse James, curious to hear what people would say. Most times about half the crowd swore they would shoot him on sight and the other half would run him for President. With opinion so contrary, how was he going to figure out whether he was a monster or a hero?

The question troubled him more and more after he got married and started having kids. His wife never liked hearing about his jobs. She told him it was bad enough worrying herself sick every minute he was away on a robbery without having to go through it all over again when he got home. But Jesse's two boys would hang around his knees and pump every last detail from him, including who was shot and who was lumped over the head. They learned their numbers by helping him count the loot on the living room floor. What was he supposed to tell these tow-haired rascals when they crawled on his lap and asked how long they had to wait before they could join the gang and become robbers?

"You'll have to wait forever," Jesse's wife would answer, "if I have anything to say about it." She wanted the boys to become auctioneers or railroad brakemen, something respectable and safe, instead of robbers. In fact she kept pestering Jesse himself to give up his murderous line of work and move to a small town somewhere and take up an innocent name and just live quietly like ordinary folks.

But Jesse liked wearing his old name, enjoyed the way it struck terror and admiration in people. The only time he felt one-hundred-percent alive was when he was riding ahead of his gang with a six-gun in his fist and a whiff of danger in the air. The gang always followed him wherever he said to go, without so much as a question. Except now and again he had a little problem with the Ford brothers, Charles and Robert, who muttered under their breath. This muttering kept on until Jesse finally told them to either speak up or shut up. Then Charles Ford said they were sick of taking orders from Jesse and they weren't any man's slaves and they wouldn't stand it anymore. Whereupon Jesse took a bullwhip and beat him to within an inch of his life. And all the while Robert looked on with eyes hard and tight like the notches in a belt. That was the last trouble Jesse had with the Ford brothers for a long time.

So no matter how much his wife begged him, he refused to give up being Jesse James. There was too much power and pleasure in wearing the name. Then one day his older boy came back from the store with bruises and cuts all over his milky dish of a face. He mumbled through swollen lips, "Some guys was standing around there eating licorice and talking about you, Daddy, and they said you was an evil man for shooting folks. So I lit into them. They was so many they whipped the stuffing out of me, but I kept telling them you *ain't* evil. And you ain't, are you, Daddy? *Are* you?"

Jesse held the boy's banged-up face in his hands and couldn't think what to say. All he could think of was himself at the same age, just turned thirteen, out in the field cultivating corn when the Federal officers came and arrested his mother for keeping a slave. And all the anger and shame of that long-ago moment swept over him again. Soon after his mother's arrest, Jesse had run away to join the Rebels as a horse thief, and he had been thieving ever since. Now he could feel the boy's heart leaning in the same direction his own heart had leaned, toward vengeance and fury, and suddenly he knew that he did not want to force that life on his own son.

"I don't know if I'm bad or good," Jesse answered at last, "but I know which one you are, and I aim to keep you that way."

Soon after that, Jesse called his gang together and told them he was retiring. Everybody took the news pretty well, except the Ford brothers, who curled their lips and gave him icy stares. "What are we supposed to do now?" Charles demanded.

"Whatever you want," Jesse replied. "Weren't you itching to be your own boss? Well, now's your chance."

The decision pleased his wife, puzzled his boys, and left Jesse himself feeling antsy. He didn't know how long he could bear to go straight. Without telling anybody except the gang, he moved his family into a blue clapboard house in St. Joseph, where nobody knew him from Adam. He grew a beard and dressed in a suit like a stuffy lawyer, with a flared coat to hide the pair of six-shooters he wore strapped around his waist. None of that was hard. But it nearly broke Jesse's heart to give up his name. He called himself Thomas Howard, a name that carried no power. Sometimes it was all he could do to keep from stopping a man in the street and telling him, "I'm Jesse James," just to see the flinch in the stranger's eye.

Every few days he walked down to the St. Joe post office and pretended to write a letter at the counter, while from the corner of his eye he watched people stopping in front of his wanted poster, with its $10,000 reward. His picture stopped them in their tracks. He could see their lips shaping his name. But nobody paid any attention to *him*, to Jesse himself, a bearded man in a frock coat writing a letter at the post office counter. If he stayed in hiding like this, how long before people would quit even blinking at his photograph? How long before they plain forgot him entirely?

It was almost a relief when the Ford brothers turned up at the house one night. Almost—but not quite, because of the cold glint in their eyes. Jesse thought of them as he thought of snakes: never turn your back if they're within biting distance. They were looking for a place to sleep and some grub to eat, to get them back on their feet for a job they were going to pull in Amazonia.

"Send them away," Jesse's wife hissed from behind the door.

But Jesse let them in. Snake-eyed or not, they knew who he was, knew what he had done.

That night his wife cried into her pillow.

"You don't need to carry on about it," said Jesse.

"I can just see it coming," she sobbed. "They're going to drag you back into that old life."

"No, they won't either. I give it up for the boys' sake, and what I swear to do, I do." But even as he lay there in bed saying that, he was itching to ride, to break loose from this quiet life and go strike terror in some poky town. "So dry up those tears, now, and quit your fretting."

She wiped her cheeks with the pillowcase. He thought of the farm wife dabbing at her eyes with the green bandanna. All these crying women. She got up and went to lock the bedroom door.

Jesse propped himself on his elbow. "What are you doing that for?"

"To keep them from sneaking in here and killing you in your sleep."

"Why ever would they want to kill me?"

"For the ten thousand dollars your corpse is worth."

He slapped the pistols that were hanging from the bed-post. "They know better than to try."

She lay without talking, but he could feel her body clenched up tight. He was a long while in drifting off.

Days passed, and the Ford brothers stayed on, eating Jesse's bread and sleeping in his extra bed. When his boys were off to school and his wife was off to the store, Jesse talked with

Robert and Charles about old times, a shoot-up here and a stickup there, and he advised them about the job they were planning on the Amazonia bank. They spoke with tight lips and never quit watching him. Jesse never took off his guns. He knew he should throw the Fords out, but so long as they stayed, in their cautious, snaky eyes he was still Jesse James.

One afternoon the older boy came home from school with a picture he had drawn for Jesse. It showed a man dressed all in black and galloping on horseback with a smoking pistol in his upraised fist. The title across the bottom read, "Jesse James rides again!" All through supper Jesse kept it on the table beside his plate, where he could admire it. He kept asking the Ford brothers what they thought of it. They slid their eyes over the picture and grunted. As soon as the dishes were cleared away he held it against the wall above the fireplace, then above the sofa, then beside the door, trying where it would look the best.

"You can't have that out where folks will look at it," said his wife.

"And why not? What's wrong with Thomas Howard admiring Jesse James?"

She stuck out her lower lip and let loose a burst of air that lifted the bangs from her forehead. Then she stamped into the kitchen.

"What do you think of it here, boys?" said Jesse, holding the picture against the wall.

"Hang it over the fireplace," said Charles Ford.

"Yeah," said Robert, "up high where everybody can see it."

"Now you're talking," said Jesse. He put some tacks in his mouth, pushed a chair onto the hearth, and reached over the mantel. "How's that?"

"Higher," said Robert.

"More to your left," said Charles.

Leaning over, pulled off center by the heavy pistols around his waist, Jesse began to lose his balance. "No sense in breaking my neck," he said. He stepped down, unstrapped the pistols and slung them over the back of the chair, then climbed back up, the picture in his outstretched arms. He was that man in black, gun smoking, eyes glaring. A wicked man, or a saint? Jesse still did not know the answer, and he was feeling the old shiver of doubt when he heard behind him the click of a hammer drawing back, the voices of his two sons crying, "Papa!" and he was just spinning around, thinking, No, no I'm not ready, I don't know the truth yet, when he saw, in the last crashing instant, the trembling barrel of Robert Ford's gun.

Ballad of
the Boll Weevil

[TRADITIONAL]

Oh, the boll weevil is a little black bug,
Come from Mexico, they say,
Come all the way to Texas, just a-looking for a place to stay,
Just a-looking for a home, just a-looking for a home.

The first time I seen the boll weevil,
He was a-setting on the square.
Next time I seen the boll weevil, he had all of his family there.
Just a-looking for a home, just a-looking for a home.

The farmer say to the weevil:
"What make your head so red?"
The weevil say to the farmer, "It's a wonder I ain't dead,
A-looking for a home, just a-looking for a home."

The farmer take the boll weevil,
And he put him in the hot sand.
The weevil say, "This is mighty hot but I'll stand it like a man,
This'll be my home, it'll be my home."

The farmer take the boll weevil,
And he put him in a lump of ice;
The boll weevil say to the farmer, "This is mighty cool and nice,
It'll be my home, this'll be my home."

The farmer take the boll weevil,
And he put him in the fire.
The boll weevil say to the farmer, "Here I are, here I are,
This'll be my home, this'll be my home."

The farmer say to the missus,
"What do you think of that?
The boll weevil done make a nest in my best Sunday hat,
Going to have a home, going to have a home."

The boll weevil say to the farmer,
"You better leave me alone.
I done eat all your cotton, now I'm going to start on your corn,
I'll have a home, I'll have a home."

The merchant got half the cotton,
The boll weevil got the rest.
Didn't leave the farmer's wife but one old cotton dress,
And it's full of holes, it's full of holes.

The farmer say to the merchant,
"We's in an awful fix.
The boll weevil ate all the cotton up and left us only sticks,
We's got no home, we's got no home."

One springtime down in Mexico two little bitty weevil bugs got married and wanted to set up house, but there wasn't a single free cotton boll in that whole country. They tramped from one field to the next, and every place they looked was already jampacked with wiggly black weevils. So they loaded their stuff and hitched a ride in a wagon and rolled on up north into Texas.

"Whooee, baby!" cried Mister Weevil when he got a peek at Texas. Rows of cotton stretched from where he stood all the way to the edge of the sky, and not another bug in sight. "Now I know what the Good Book means when it talks about the promised land. Right here it is! Land of milk and honey!"

Missus Weevil said, "Quit wagging your jaw and get this stuff unloaded while I pick us out a place to live."

He puffed along behind her, dragging the satchels and gunnysacks across that field. By and by she found a likely plant, shinnied up the stalk, drilled a hole in the cotton boll with her long pointy snout, and laid her eggs. The two of them settled down to housekeeping.

Next day they were lazing around on a leaf, soaking up sunshine and waiting on those eggs to hatch, when a discouraged-looking, red-skinned man in blue duck overalls came along the row chopping weeds. His name was Luke, straight out of the Bible. "Uh, oh," he said, spying Mister and Missus Weevil, "little black cooties. That sure don't look good." He stooped down until his nose almost brushed the plant. Like the rest of his face, his nose was burned the color of peanut skins. "I better mash them before they eat this cotton all up." He lifted the hoe to strike.

Mister ran and hid, but Missus reared on her hind legs and said to the man, "Hold your horses! Don't you go mashing innocent folks until you hear what I got to say."

Luke squinched up his face in wonderment. Always willing to take a rest, he put down the hoe and leaned on the handle. "Talk ahead, Mizz Bug."

"First off," she said, "is this here your cotton?"

"No, it ain't. Do I look like I own a thing in the world? This here cotton and field and the whole blessed place belongs to the farmer that lives up in the big white house. All I do is work it for him. And he told me to kill every bug I see."

"He couldn't be talking about weevils, because we just rode up from Mexico and we're the first ones that ever set foot in Texas. Nobody around here even laid eyes on us before. Did this boss of yours say to go murdering *weevils?*"

"No, ma'am. He ain't said nothing about weevils."

"All right, then. We're just poor folks looking for a home. Anything wrong with that?"

"I reckon not," Luke answered.

"You got a home?" said Missus Weevil.

"You might call it that. The boss loans me a shack to live in so long as I work his fields."

"If he loans you a whole shack, he won't mind us living in one measly old cotton boll, will he? Poor folks got to stick together. You hear what I'm saying?"

"I hear you." Luke gave a shrug, then moseyed on down the row, chopping weeds.

By the time he worked his way past that spot again a few weeks later, there were about fifty thousand baby weevils already hatched and grown and married up and moved out to lay eggs and keep house in their own cotton bolls. He took one look around—cooties on every plant as far as he could see—and knew he never should have listened to that teeninchy Mizz Bug. Off he ran to fetch the boss.

The farmer came lickety-split. He was a skinny man, swaybacked and curved like a pump handle, and he wore a straw hat that would have covered a bushelbasket. When he saw those fifty thousand weevils chewing on his cotton, he shook so hard he set the brim of his hat flopping like the wings of a buzzard. "What in blazes *are* they, Luke?" he cried.

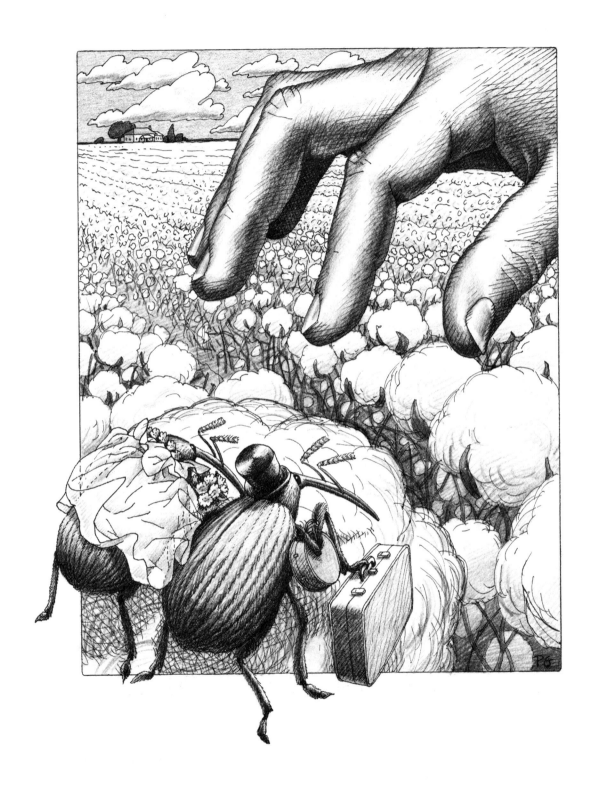

"Beats me, boss," Luke answered. He scratched an ear with the hoe handle, then added casually, "Seems like I heard somebody say weevils."

"Weevils? Rhymes with *evils*. Where in tarnation did they come from?"

Luke scratched the other ear. "Seems like I heard somebody say Mexico, boss."

The farmer pinched one of the bugs between his fingers, put it in the palm of his hand, and lifted it up close to his eyes. And who should it be but Missus, the mother and grandmother and umpty-great-grandmother of all the weevils in Texas.

She twitched her feelers and said, "How do, farmer?"

"*Do?*" the farmer yelled. "I'll tell you how I do. I've never done worse in my life. Lookit here, half my field's ruined. And all on account of you ugly bugs. What business have you got coming in here and eating up my cotton?"

"We're just looking for a place to live, like every other critter in creation," said Missus. "Do you grudge us a couple acres of your cotton?"

"*Acres!* I grudge you so much as one square inch!" The farmer was so mad he started hopping.

Luke backed down the row a safe distance. "You tell them, boss. Don't let any little black cooties put it over on you."

"No, I won't," the farmer agreed. "I'm going to kill every last one, beginning with you," he said to Missus, bringing his thumb down fast to squash her. But she was even faster. She skinned off his hand like a shot and jumped into the nearest cotton bush. The farmer bent over, hunting for her, but everywhere he looked it was solid weevils. So he took off his hat and began whacking left and right until he wore out both arms and had to sit down for a breather. When he went to fan himself with the hat, there was a family of weevils inside building a nest. He moaned, "O Lordy, whatever are we going to *do*, Luke?"

"Beats me, boss," Luke said.

"I know," said the farmer after a spell. "Seeing as how they come from Mexico, where it's hotter than a tin roof in the sunshine, let's freeze them out."

So they hauled wagonloads of ice to the field and set it down in the weevily cotton. "That ought to fix them," said the farmer.

But the weevils swam around in the puddles of ice water and kicked their legs and sighed with pleasure. They hadn't been that cool for a long while.

"Now what?" said the farmer. Before he could think what to do next, a hundred thousand weevils hatched out and ate up their cotton bolls and moved on to fresh plants.

In a little while he snapped his fingers and declared, "I got it for sure this time, Luke. We'll burn them out."

Luke and the farmer dragged brush to the field, laid it in a circle around the ruined cotton, and set it alight. In about a minute the weevils packed up their stuff and trooped to the far end of the field and set up house again.

The farmer sat down and cried. Luke stood by and clucked his tongue. Everywhere around, the weevils drilled holes and laid eggs and hatched babies and gobbled cotton. At last the farmer sighed, "There isn't a thing a man can do, you know that, Luke? Not a blessed thing."

"Sure don't seem like it, boss," Luke agreed.

The farmer owed money to the banker for his land, to the doctor for medicine, to the merchant for seed, and to the preacher for dues in church. As soon as word reached town about the ruined cotton, the banker came running, and not far behind him came the other three.

"I get the land," said the banker.

"I get the house," said the doctor.

"I get the wagon and horses and plow," said the merchant.

"I get whatever good cotton is left," said the preacher.

Missus heard them talking right outside her nest. She poked her nose out and said, "You got the short end of the stick, preacher, because we aim to eat all the cotton."

The preacher steamed. "And why would you do a wicked thing like that?"

"Nothing wicked about it. We're just poor folks looking for a place to live. Haven't you read your Bible? Don't you remember where it says about the meek inheriting the earth?"

"You hear that little bug?" the preacher asked the other men. "If they're going to ruin all the cotton, then I get the horses."

"Nosirree," the merchant insisted, "those horses are mine."

"Then I'll take the house," said the preacher.

"Oh, no, you don't," said the doctor. "My wife's been wanting that house for years, and I'm going to have it."

"Then I guess I'll have to take the land," the preacher declared.

"Guess again," said the banker.

The four men were still squabbling when Missus told Mister it was time to move on to a new field, since this one was all used up. So he packed the bags and followed her on down the road. About three million other weevils tagged along, and spread out over the next farm. Pretty soon that farm was gobbled up, and the next one and the next. On they went, a hundred million weevils, a billion, a trillion, more weevils than raindrops in a cloudburst.

Meanwhile the farmer moved into the shack and threw Luke out into the dirt. "I hate to do it," said the farmer, "but everybody needs a home, and this is the only one I've got left."

"I hear what you're saying, boss," said Luke. He tied up his things in a bundle, tied the bundle onto his hoe, put the hoe over his shoulder, and trudged on east looking for work. But Texas was all full of weevils, and so was Louisiana, Mississippi, Alabama, Georgia—every single place he tried—so Luke just kept walking, mile after mile, year after year, and never a place to lay his head.

The Johnson Boys

[TRADITIONAL]

Johnson boys was raised in the ashes,
Never knew how to court a maid.
Turn their backs and hide their faces,
Sight of a pretty girl makes them afraid.

Shame, oh, shame on the Johnson boys!

Johnson boys, they went a-courting,
The Coon Creek girls, so pretty and sweet.
They couldn't make no conversation,
They didn't know where to put their feet.

Johnson boys, they went a-hunting,
Took two dogs and went astray.
Tore their clothes and scratched their faces,
Didn't get home till the break of day.

Johnson boys, went to the city,
Riding in a Chevrolet.
They came back all broke and a-walking,
Had no money for to pay their way.

Johnson boys eat peas and honey,
They been doing it all of their life.
Makes the peas taste mighty funny,
But it keeps them on the knife.

It was bone-dry in Oklahoma the year the Johnson boys were born. Nothing green would grow. Mr. Johnson's scrawny bulls quit going to the pasture and leaned against the barn in despair. His bees left their hives and flew away in search of a place where flowers still bloomed. Whirlwinds loaded with dust roared by the house like freight trains. Rattlesnakes and coyotes slunk up to the kitchen door with their tongues hanging out, begging for a drink. Mrs. Johnson wanted to shoot the varmints on sight; but Mr. Johnson—

who was tenderhearted and addlebrained, in her opinion—set out pans of water for them to drink. Each day, more thirsty critters appeared at the doorstep.

"It's all very well for you to surround the house with murdersome beasts," Mrs. Johnson complained. "You aren't the one that's going to deliver her first baby out here in this howling desert and not a doctor within fifty miles." She was from Oklahoma City, and never missed a chance of reminding her husband that she was too delicate for life in the country.

"Leave me be," he answered, pumping a bucket of water for the newly arrived armadillos and jack rabbits. "You think I'm five kinds of fool, but I know what I'm doing."

Late in that dry summer, much to her surprise, Mrs. Johnson delivered not only her first child but her second one as well, two boys with spindly bodies and bright red hair. They looked to her like a pair of flaming matches fitted with arms and legs. The first one she called William, and the second one—who came along twenty minutes later—she called Darrell, borrowing the names from two uncles who used to carry her piggyback when she was a girl. At first the only way she could tell them apart was by smell, the older one having a whiff of cinnamon, the younger one a hint of cloves.

When Bill and Darrell opened their mouths to let loose their first cry, dust blew in and covered their tongues with the taste of ashes. They clammed shut right away. From that day forward, until they both died on the same afternoon eighty-seven years later, the Johnson twins never opened their mouths any more than necessary. As babies, they hardly ever bawled.

As boys and grown men they rarely spoke, paying out each word stingily, as if it were a coin.

Even as babies, they hardly ate enough to keep a toad alive. It was a good thing, too, because as soon as they outgrew their mama's milk, what they had to eat, mostly, were the raccoons and coyotes and other varmints their pappy shot from the doorstep. Every time Mr. Johnson brought in a snake or a four-legger for the cookpot, he made a point of telling Mrs. Johnson, "Now ain't you glad I put out that water? Don't I know which end is up?"

She never bothered to answer his brags. In the city, where she came from, people did not have to eat boiled skunk and roasted owl. They went to the store and bought real food in cans and boxes.

Dry as it was, Mr. Johnson could not make a living from cattle or honeybees. His bulls looked like clothes racks with cowhides slung over them. His beehives sat empty in the meadow, like tilted white grave markers. So he ordered two dozen crates of patent medicine from Boston, loaded it in his old spinach-colored Chevrolet, and set off to peddle his cures on the back roads. As soon as Bill and Darrell got enough starch in their backbones to sit upright on the car seat, they rode along with him on these peddling trips. Mrs. Johnson was glad to have them out from underfoot, her nerves were so frazzled. At every farmhouse and cabin, Mr. Johnson sauntered up and banged on the door. No matter what strangers poked their noses out, he talked with them as if he were their oldest friend in the world. Every time this happened, Bill and Darrell's faces turned as red as their hair. They crawled into the back seat and hid while Pappy exchanged life histories with these strangers. More often than not, the people bought a can of salve or a bottle of elixir. The boys noticed, from listening through the open window to Pappy's sales pitch, that a medicine good for arthritis at one farm might be good for jaundice or pneumonia at the next one.

"I call it my rubber medicine," he told the boys when they were rolling again. "It will stretch to cover any ailment under the sun."

Riding between houses, he taught them their alphabet and numbers. They wrote with chalk on the back of a skillet, and erased their mistakes with licked thumbs. Since Mr. Johnson followed his own notions of spelling and arithmetic—notions which nobody else shared—the boys learned to write and cipher in mysterious ways. Later, books proved to be hard nuts to crack, for the words inside were spelled according to the dictionary, not according to Mr. Johnson.

"Books is all dead knowledge, anyhow," he advised the boys. "I never read one in my life, and look how far I got. Travel the roads and visit with folks, that's where you pick up your living knowledge!"

Bill and Darrell traveled enough to be wiser than Solomon. They saw half of Oklahoma from the seat of Pappy's medicine car. But they hardly even spoke to Pappy, let alone to strangers. Between themselves they communicated in a silent language of curled lips, raised eyebrows, gesturing fingers. All they had to do was exchange a glance, and each one knew what the other was thinking.

Pappy figured his sons were short a few marbles. "They're

harmless as woodchucks," he would tell strangers who happened to notice Bill and Darrell gawking from the back seat of the car. "They just ain't one hundred percent in the upstairs, is all."

The twins were thirteen years old when they came home from a peddling tour to find Mrs. Johnson slumped over the kitchen table, dead of snakebite. There was a scrawled note beside her, saying, "I told you so, you and your murdersome beasts!"

Not long after, Pappy broke out in a pox that none of his cure-alls would touch. With his last breath he told the boys, "Keep on selling medicine. When you get up a few years older, find you a pair of country girls to marry. Don't even look at a city girl. Remember all the wisdom I taught you." Then Pappy died, too.

Bill and Darrell moped around the house for a few days, not saying a word. Every time one of them cranked himself up to mutter a sentence, he would look over and see that the other one already knew what he was about to say; so they both kept quiet. They took stock of the farm: one bull, two dogs, three mules—all of them bony and low-spirited—a dozen empty beehives, a leaky barn, a rattly car, a two-room house, and forty acres of Oklahoma dust. They soon ate the bull. Neither had much stomach for mule or dog. With guns across their knees, they sat for hours inside the kitchen door, waiting for a varmint to approach the dish of water they had left on the stoop; but over the years the beasts had grown wise to Pappy's trick, and not a one came anywhere close.

So one morning the brothers decided to go hunting in the

woods. They grabbed the shotguns, chose the dog with the longest nose, and set out. Before they had walked very far the air split open with a mournful howl. Bill and Darrell threw one another a scared look, their hair standing up on end like red seaweed, and they spun around and galloped for home. The howling got louder as they neared the house. They were almost in the yard before they realized the noise was coming from the dog they had left chained to the gatepost.

Next day they went hunting again, this time with both dogs. Crossing the fields they shot at crows, squirrels, and lizards, but never hit a thing. On the edge of the woods, the dogs snuffled around, caught a scent, then took off yapping, and in about half a minute they were beyond earshot. The brothers called and called, but no dogs. They crept forward into the woods all by their lonesome. Every now and again they stopped, played statue, and listened. Nothing but wind and bird song. Then just before sundown, way deep in the woods, everything quiet, all of a sudden here came a heavy thrashing noise through the undergrowth, charging straight at them.

"Wolf!" cried Bill.

"Bear!" cried Darrell.

It was a rare disagreement. Instead of arguing, they flung down their shotguns and started running, side by side, huffing and gasping, each one thinking the other knew the way home. In two minutes they were lost. Meanwhile, the dogs, which had made all that ruckus in the undergrowth, trailed along behind them. About midnight the dogs got tired and went on back to the house; but Darrell and Bill—all scratched up from the briers and their clothes in tatters—did not find their way home until daybreak.

Hunting was no good. So they decided to try Pappy's advice and go back on the road selling medicine. They avoided the old places where they had gone with him. What if people recognized the spinach-green Chevrolet, came outside, and started asking them questions about Pappy? The brothers turned red just thinking about having to answer. They drove and drove until they came to houses they had never seen before. Whenever they stopped, Bill would poke Darrell in the ribs, then Darrell would poke Bill, but neither would get out of the car, let alone march up to the door and knock. It was going to be hard selling medicine if they never even *saw* anybody.

The thing to do, they decided, was to drive into Oklahoma City and park and let folks walk up to *them*. Back home they took some barn paint and spelled out—according to Pappy's method—MEDSIN 4 SAL in red letters a foot high along both flanks of the Chevrolet. Before the paint was dry they were already in a sweat, just thinking about all the traffic in the city. They figured maybe they'd better practice in a town first. So they drove into Coon Creek, rolled to a stop in the middle of the main street—the only street—and waited for something terrible to happen. Nothing much happened at all. Every few minutes another car came along, swerved around them, and kept going. Every little while somebody sauntered by, glanced in through the windshield, and moseyed on past.

Darrell was moved to say, "Town ain't so bad."

"Not half so bad as Pappy made it out to be," said Bill.

Following these speeches, they rested. Then, growing bolder, they practiced backing up, pulling into driveways, and making U-turns. Everything went fine until they swung too far in a turn and ran up onto a lawn and lurched to a halt with the Chevrolet's bumper mashed against the porch railing of a tall blue house. Two girls with matching round pink faces and mud-colored hair blinked down at them from rockers on the porch. After the surprise wore off, the girls jumped to their feet, rushed down from the porch to the car, one on each side, and started jabbering. The brothers rolled up the windows, but the girls only raised their voices.

"Well, howdy, there. What a way to come calling! How'd you hear about us? We've never seen you in Coon Creek before. My land, what red hair you've got! Of course you'll have to talk with Daddy before you can take us riding. Is this your very own car? Why'd you mess it up with painting all over it? What's them boxes in the back seat? And look at your patchy overalls! You ought to dress up finer before you come visit ladies!"

Bill and Darrell were both fumbling at the gearshift and stomping at the clutch, trying to get the car in reverse. Finally they succeeded, and roared backward off the lawn. As soon as they hit the street they shifted into first and peeled for home, watched all the while by the pair of shocked pink faces.

"If that's what courting's like," said Bill, "I done had all of it I care for."

"Me, too," said Darrell.

By and by they got up their nerve to drive into Oklahoma City. They had never been there before, since Pappy thought it was seven times worse than Sodom and Gomorrah rolled together, but all they had to do was follow the signs. The first shacks they came to looked about like country places, only thrown closer together. As they rolled deeper into the city, the buildings got taller, streets shot in from both sides, cars and trucks ran every which way in thick herds, lights overhead kept changing from red to green to yellow to red, people jammed along the sidewalks thicker than cows at milking time, storefronts and signs whipped by, horns blared. Even though Bill and Darrell swiveled their heads back and forth like owls to stare through every window, they could not take it all in, and neither one saw the lamppost rise in front of them until the Chevrolet rammed into it. The hood sprang open and steam gushed from the radiator. People started crowding up to the car, their faces burst wide with shouts. Before the circle closed, the twins leapt out and shoved their way clear and ran down the street as hard as they could go, dodging cars and never looking back.

That was the last they ever saw of the Chevrolet or Pappy's patent medicine—or Oklahoma City, for that matter. It took them four days to walk home.

"I ain't never budging from this place again," said Darrell.

"Me, neither," said Bill.

The cupboard was still bare, so they ate one of the mules. This left them two for plowing, if only the ground were wet enough to grow a crop. They were trying to decide which of the dogs to eat first when the sky turned black and rain came down. It kept on coming, day after day, night after night. The boys put out every bucket they could find. They hitched a scraper behind the mules and dug a pond. When it was filled they threw off their clothes and dived in, red hair blazing, like a pair of skinny-legged matches that no amount of water could put out.

Soon after the storm passed on east toward Arkansas, the meadow lit up with flowers. Bill and Darrell were standing in it, knee-deep in color, mouths hanging open, when a swarm of bees came snarling past. The bees scrawled an inky trail against the sky, landed in a knot on one of Pappy's hives, and disappeared inside. Darrell put on Pappy's old bee hat, with its dangling net, and Bill rigged a hat for himself out of a Stetson and some window screen. Side by side they stooped down and peered into the hive where the swarm had settled. Every bee seemed to know what it was up to, yet the only sound was an absent-minded hum, like Pappy going over old tunes. At that moment the brothers understood what they had been called into this world to do, which was to raise bees and make honey. That is what they did, for the next seventy years. The sign they put on the road said HUNNY, but everybody knew what it meant, and people drove from all over the state to buy bottled sweetness from the silent Johnson boys.

Buffalo Skinners

[TRADITIONAL]

'Twas in the town of Jacksboro in the spring of seventy-three,
A man by the name of Crego came stepping up to me,
Saying, "How do you do, young fellow, and how would you like to go
And spend the summer pleasantly on the range of the buffalo?"

"It's me being out of employment," this to Crego I did say,
"This going out on the buffalo range depends upon the pay.
But if you'll pay good wages and transportation too,
I think, sir, I will go with you to the range of the buffalo."

"Yes, I will pay good wages, give transportation too,
Provided you will go with me and stay the summer through.
But if you should grow homesick, come back to Jacksboro,
I won't pay transportation from the range of the buffalo."

It's now our outfit was complete—seven able-bodied men,
With navy six and needle gun—our troubles did begin.
Our way it was a pleasant one, the route we had to go,
Until we crossed Pease River on the range of the buffalo.

It's now we've crossed Pease River, our troubles have begun.
The first damned tail I went to rip, Christ! how I cut my thumb!
While skinning the damned old stinkers our lives wasn't a show,
For the Indians watched to pick us off while skinning the buffalo.

He fed us on such sorry chuck I wished myself most dead,
It was old jerked beef, croton coffee, and sour bread.
Pease River's as salty as hellfire, the water I could never go—
O God! I wished I had never come to the range of the buffalo.

Our meat it was buffalo hump and iron-wedge bread,
And all we had to sleep on was a buffalo robe for bed.
The fleas and gray-backs worked on us, O boys, it was not slow,
I'll tell you there's no worse hell on earth than the range of the buffalo.

Our hearts were cased with buffalo hocks, our souls were cased with steel,
And the hardships of that summer would nearly make us reel.
While skinning the damned old stinkers our lives they had no show,
For the Indians waited to pick us off on the hills of Mexico.

The season being near over, old Crego he did say,
The crowd had been extravagant, was in debt to him that day.
We coaxed him and we begged him and still it was no go—
We left old Crego's bones to bleach on the range of the buffalo.

Oh, it's now we've crossed Pease River and homeward we are bound,
No more in that hellfired country shall ever we be found.
Go home to our wives and sweethearts, tell others not to go,
For God's forsaken the buffalo range and the damned old buffalo.

*I*n the spring of seventy-three, not one cattle drive was rumbling anywhere in Texas. Last year's herds of longhorns were still pawing dirt at the railheads in Kansas and Nebraska. Some drovers said the northern ranchers were behind it all, trying to ruin the free-roaming cowpokes. Others blamed the railroads. Some claimed that folks back East were fed up with beef. Others said, naw, you couldn't ever fill up those easterners, they were bottomless pits; they'd buy every longhorn Texas could deliver, if only the bankers weren't sitting on all the money.

In Jacksboro that spring the cowboys knew one thing for sure—they were out of work. They slouched against storefronts, picked fights, tossed knives, chewed the stems of long grasses. Their pockets and bellies were empty, and the pants sagged over their haunches.

"No moos on the move, boys, no work for us buckaroos," was how Chief Mitchell summed things up.

Chief earned his nickname from looking like an Indian. His hair was long and straight and blacker than the inside of a cookpot at midnight. The bones of his cheeks looked like fists balled up under the skin. His eyes, dark and shiny, could have been rocks at the bottom of a creek. His skin, though, was as white as cotton. The sun never turned it dark. Looking at that pale skin, the other cowboys figured it was safe to call him Chief. Nobody would ever take him for a real Indian. The truth was, they could have taken him for an Indian and been half right, because his mother was a Comanche. But that was a dark secret Chief never told another living soul.

The Comanches had raised him until he was eleven, when his mother died, and then his father had sent him to live among white people. Now he was twenty, and in his heart he was neither white nor Indian. The only place he felt at home was out on the trail, on the back of a pony. He was tall, and if his legs had not been so bowed he would have been three inches taller. A long drink of water, his friends liked to say. Water was about all he could afford to drink these days, with nothing in his pockets except a mashed bullet that had been dug out of his shoulder by a blacksmith in Fort Worth.

"I'm so hard up for a job," Chief said, "I'd hire on with Moses to part the Red Sea."

"You tell them, Chief."

"I'd chop down George Washington's cherry tree and take the blame," he said.

"Say it, Chief, say it."

He and six of Jacksboro's hungriest cowboys were dawdling in the Heartbreak Saloon one afternoon, pushing sawdust around on the floor with the pointy toes of their boots,
hoping somebody with cash would blunder in and buy them
supper, when through the door came a trail boss named Crego.

"Howdy, boys," Crego announced.

The cowboys threw wolfish glances at him. "You buying?"
one of them said.

Crego loosed a wheezy laugh, showing a mouthful of yellow teeth. "Do I look like I'm made of money?"

The cowboys turned away and pretended he wasn't there.
Just about everybody in the saloon had driven cattle for Crego
once, but nobody had done it twice. He was a slippery man
with a face like a rag dipped in grease and crumpled up and
laid out in the sun to crack. He had a lizard's narrow jaw
and cold green eyes. Summer and winter, in town and on the
trail, he wore a battered top hat, a swallow-tailed coat of black
wool, a plaid vest, a shirt that used to be white, and a droopy
bow tie.

"Any hombre in here want a job?" he said.

Now the cowboys swung around. Six of them flung up their
arms, shouting, "Right here! I'm your man!" not caring if it
was Crego making the offer, they were so eager for work.

But Chief narrowed his eyes and asked, "Job doing what?"

"Killing buffalo," said Crego.

Not a man in the room knew the first thing about killing
buffalo, except Chief, who used to ride along and watch, as
a boy, when the Comanche braves hunted the great lumbering beasts. He knew that shooting one was like trying to stop

a landslide. And he also knew that, for his mother's people, buffalo were holy. He turned his creek-pebble eyes on Crego. "How're you going to sell buffalo meat when you can't sell beef?"

"I'm not after meat," said Crego, "I'm after hides. Uncle Sam's paying a bounty on tails. Wants to starve out the Indians, so they'll slink onto the reservations like pussycats."

Chief listened with a face as blank as a board. The other cowboys huddled around him and mulled this over. Hunting buffalo was not their line of work, and Crego was not their kind of boss. But a job was a job. Finally they shoved Chief forward as spokesman, and he asked, "What kind of wages are you paying?"

"Top dollar," said Crego.

"Whereabouts we going?"

"Panhandle."

Several of the men whistled.

Chief said, "That's Kiowa and Comanche hunting grounds."

"Who says? They got a sign on it saying they own it? Now don't tell me you boys would let a few savages scare you off some good money." Crego slid his eyes over them like a lizard on a hot rock watching flies. "Listen, now, I'll even pay wages for the time it takes us riding there and back. I'll supply bullets, new Winchesters, grub, everything. The only condition is," he said, drawing a matchstick from his vest and scraping his yellow teeth, "you've got to stay with me through the summer to the first of September. If you get worn out or lovesick for your sweethearts and put your tail between your legs and sneak home early, you won't get a dime."

"We'll finish whatever we start," said one cowboy.

Chief said nothing. He did not want to kill buffalo, did not want to help drive Kiowa and Comanches onto reservations. But he needed work, and if he did not go another man would. So he saddled his pony.

They headed north, Crego in front driving the chuck wagon, the seven cowpokes behind on their ponies. There was no cook. To save money, Crego fixed the meals himself. He saved a few bucks on the food, too. For most of a week they ate beef jerky and sourdough bread, drank coffee made from spurge beans, swallowed it all down with a helping of dust. The beef was so tough they had to snag it between their teeth and saw it off with a knife.

"As soon as we get to the buffalo range," Crego promised them, "we'll eat tongue and liver and roasted hump. We'll drink sweet water from the creeks."

The first water they came to, the Pease River, was bitter with salt. Chief burned his lips from drinking it. He was hoping they never would see a buffalo, never see a Comanche, and Crego would have to pay them for riding out and back and sleeping under the stars. But north of the Pease, where the land rose and dipped like a brown ocean, they began to pass gleaming white buffalo skulls along the trail, then old droppings, then fresh ones. Finally they spied a herd moving in a black knot over a distant swell.

"Go for them, boys!" Crego shouted.

You hire on to do a job, and you do a job, Chief thought, as he whipped his pony into a gallop. The other cowboys did the same, and the seven of them were soon closing on the buffalo. Pretending they were old hands at this business, they rode straight ahead, lowered their Winchesters, and fired into the herd. Not a beast fell. None even slowed down, and in two minutes the last shaggy back disappeared over a hill.

When Crego drove the wagon up to where the buckaroos waited, he was fuming. "Some hunters! Shoot off five dollars' worth of shells and don't kill a single buffalo! Don't you know you got to ride up alongside them close enough almost to grab their horns, and you got to shoot them through the lungs?"

"Where the devil is their lungs *at?*" one cowboy asked.

"Right behind their shoulder," said Crego. "Shoot them anywhere else, and you might as well be throwing pebbles."

"Whyn't you show us how it's done," Chief suggested.

Crego bared his yellow teeth. "Because that's what I hired you hombres for."

They soon had a chance to try out Crego's advice. They topped a rise, and the valley beyond was filled with a black tide—buffalo as far as they could see. Again they dashed forward, only this time each man picked out a beast and took after it and held his fire as long as he dared. Chief trailed a bull that looked twice as big and twice as mean as a longhorn. He wrapped his legs tight around the pony in case it shied, gripped the bridle in one hand, rifle in the other, and when he got within a few yards he sang out an old prayer, then fired. No change in the buffalo. He fired again. Now the bull swerved, head lowered, and made straight for him. The pony leapt aside. Chief clung to the saddle and kept firing. After half a dozen shots the buffalo swung away and thundered off into a ravine.

Chief drew rein, his heart pounding from being so close

to the bull. It is a medicine beast, he thought. Not meant for killing.

"Hey, cowboy," Crego yelled at him, "you think you're on a Sunday school picnic? Kick up that pony and ride!"

Chief glared back at the trail boss. He picked out another buffalo, this one a cow that somebody must have hit, she was limping so. He drove the pony up against her flank before shooting—once, twice—and the cow staggered to a halt, tottered like a drunk, then keeled over. Chief jumped down, put a foot on her ribs, and let out a shaky yell. He gashed his thumb while cutting off her tail, but he sucked the blood and still felt good.

That night in camp they ate hump roast and raw liver and sucked marrow from the leg bones. They had killed and skinned nine buffalo. Crego figured they had used up one hundred and seventeen bullets. "We got to do better than that, boys, or the hides'll cost me more than I make off them."

Nine buffalo, Chief thought, licking grease from his lips and staring across the dark plain. What do the Comanches eat tonight?

Next day they killed twelve; the day after, seventeen. The first week they skinned over a hundred. "That's more like it," Crego murmured. He wrote the numbers in a shabby ledger book. Every few days he drove a wagonload of hides to Fort Elliott.

After only two weeks, Chief had got his fill of buffalo hunting. Stories about the great holy beasts kept rising in his memory, stories and songs and prayers, words from his

mother's people. Every time he killed one and skinned it and left the carcass to rot on the plain, he felt ashamed.

Pretty soon the other cowboys were also fed up with hunting buffalo. Any minute one of those brutes could hook his horns in your pony's belly or knock you to the ground and trample you, and all the while you're looking ahead for gullies to fall in and watching behind for Indians. When the sun didn't blister you the rain drove nails through your skin. The fleas and black flies swarmed over you from the mangy hides and never gave you a second's peace. It was a long sight from herding poky cattle along the Chisholm Trail.

At dusk, Chief curled up in a buffalo robe beside the campfire, shut his eyes, and tumbled into nightmares. Time and again he woke up sweating because in his dreams a bull was charging at him, or his mother's people were gathering in a circle and demanding to know why he was slaughtering their four-legged brothers and sisters, or wolves were picking over his bones.

Real wolves crept through camp, sniffing the fresh hides. Packs of them snarled over the buffalo carcasses. Whatever the wolves left, the turkey buzzards and black vultures finished. As the hunters worked their way across the North Texas plains, whenever Chief turned in his saddle to look back he would see the scattered bodies, black with vultures or gray with wolves. What were his mother's people eating?

One cowboy quit in July, another in August. Crego refused to give either man a dime. "The deal was," he reminded them, "either stay all summer or lose your pay."

Chief and the other four hands stuck it out. They got sick

of drinking salty water, sick of eating buffalo, sick of gnawing iron-hard bread. They were bruised, bitten, cut up, and worn down. But they stayed on until a change in weather told them September had come, and then they asked Crego for their pay.

He had just returned from hauling a load of skins to Fort Elliott. According to a calendar at the fort, he said, it was still August, too early to quit.

"It's a week or more into September," Chief insisted, and the other cowboys backed him up.

Then Crego said, well, maybe it was. But they had run up so many expenses—what with grub and bullets, two guns broken, four ponies killed, a new wheel for the wagon—that he could not afford to pay them.

Chief waited for the man's yellow teeth to show, thinking it must be a joke. But instead of smiling, Crego pulled a match from his vest and began calmly chewing on it.

So Chief said, "I don't think I heard you right."

Crego removed the match, pointed at each of them in turn, as if counting them, the way he had counted the dingy hides. "You heard me. I'm saying it cost me more to keep you boys than what I got for the buffalo you killed. As simple as that. You want to see my books?" And he drew the shabby ledger from beneath the wagon seat, opening it to a page of numbers.

"You know none of us can't figure," said Chief.

"Then you'll have to take my word for it." Crego shut the ledger, held it against his chest, and finally showed his teeth, the match jutting out like a key in a lock.

They argued with him all afternoon, coaxed him, threatened him, but he would not budge. Finally they cast looks around the circle and all five cowboys drew their guns. Chief never was sure who fired first. Before they were done everybody had a shot at Crego. They tugged his pockets out, but did not find a penny. He must have left the dough back at the fort, or hidden it somewhere on the way. It was sunset when they turned their backs on the buffalo range, leaving Crego for the wolves and buzzards and bleaching sun.

Chief told the others he had a journey to make. He rode away from them into the sun, toward the dry meatless camp of the Comanches. His heart was a great bird with a broken wing.

The other four cowboys rode back east. By the time they crossed the Pease River, they had shaken off some of their bitterness, and were laughing. Near Jacksboro they met two herds of longhorns heading north, which meant there was honest work again for cowboys.

The Dying Cowboy

[TRADITIONAL]

As I walked out in the streets of Laredo,
As I walked out in Laredo one day,
I spied a poor cowboy wrapped up in white linen,
Wrapped up in white linen and cold as the clay.

"I see by your outfit that you are a cowboy,"
These words he did say as I boldly stepped by.
"Come sit down beside me and hear my sad story—
I was shot in the breast and I know I must die.

"Let sixteen gamblers come handle my coffin,
Let sixteen cowboys come sing me a song,
Take me to the graveyard and lay the sod o'er me,
For I'm a poor cowboy and I know I've done wrong.

"It was once in the saddle I used to go dashing,
It was once in the saddle I used to go gay.
'Twas first to drinking and then to card playing,
Got shot in the breast, I am dying today.

"Get six jolly cowboys to carry my coffin,
Get six pretty girls to carry my pall.
Put bunches of roses all over my coffin,
Put roses to deaden the clods as they fall.

"O beat the drum slowly and play the fife lowly,
And play the dead march as you carry me along,
Take me to the green valley and lay the sod o'er me,
For I'm a young cowboy and I know I've done wrong."

We beat the drum slowly and played the fife lowly,
And bitterly wept as we bore him along.
For we all loved our comrade, so brave, young, and handsome,
We all loved our comrade, although he'd done wrong.

Each night when he trudged home, ink-stained and blurry-eyed, from the bank where he worked as a bookkeeper, Sherwood knocked hesitantly at the landlady's door and asked whether any packages had arrived for him. She would thrust her fierce head out, eye him up and down as if she were calculating whether he would fit in her skillet, then fling his mail at him. If what she flung at him included a box, she was sure to point out that it seemed to her mighty suspicious, a young man like him getting all this stuff. Was he counterfeiting money in his room? Was he brewing whiskey? Was he smuggling? She ran a moral house and would not put up with any shenanigans.

Sherwood backed down the hall, denying all wickedness. When he bumped against the stairs he swung around and raced up to his room, cradling the package. He unwrapped it with trembling fingers. One box held a pair of chaps, in the next was a checkered shirt with a setting sun embroidered across the back, then came spurs, a pair of boots made from alligator skin, a belt with a turquoise buckle, a string tie, a lasso. As each item arrived from the mail-order company, he tried it on and posed before the mirror. With each package, he looked more and more like a cowboy. It was as if his true self were being assembled piecemeal. Before going to bed he always locked everything away in his trunk, to hide it from the snoopy landlady.

On a card in his wallet he had an alphabetical list of the articles he had sent for, twenty-three in all. Sometimes at his desk in the bank he would pull out the card and study it. He checked off the items one by one, until only the red polka-dot bandanna was missing. When at last one evening the landlady hurled at him a fat envelope containing the bandanna, his outfit was complete. That night he dressed up in all his gear and sauntered back and forth past the mirror, glancing at himself sidelong. What he saw in the glass was so dashing, he could only bear the sight of it for a few minutes. Afterward he packed everything in the trunk, dressed in his gray bookkeeper's suit, and lay down to wait for morning. Sleep was out of the question.

Well before dawn he arose, put the week's rent on his pillow, checked in the closet and under the bed to make sure he had left nothing behind, then heaved the trunk onto his shoulder and crept down the stairs. He was terrified the landlady would rip open her door and glare at him. But as he tiptoed past he could hear the locomotive hiss of her snoring.

At the railway station he sat down to wait, draping his legs over the trunk to keep anybody from walking off with it. Having memorized the timetable, he knew without looking that the next train for Chicago left in two hours. Every few minutes he patted his right coat pocket, where his savings were stashed away, and then his left, where he kept the notebook in which he planned to make notes for his western novel. Just thinking about the West, he could hardly keep still. The landlady would have to find another boarder to pick on. The bank would have to get along without him. He was through with Cleveland.

On the train he unfolded the map over his knees and traced with his finger the route to Laramie, Wyoming. The path was dark from all the previous times he had traced it. More than a year earlier, after comparing the towns in a hundred westerns, he had picked out Laramie as the most promising site for his research. He kept opening and closing the notebook, but resisted the temptation of writing anything in it until after he had left Chicago and had crossed the Mississippi River at Quincy. Now he was in the West. But it still looked an awful lot like Ohio. So he kept licking his pencil and gazing out the window, but held off writing. Near Topeka, where he changed trains, he saw a herd of cattle, and wrote that down: *Broody steers enshrouded in dust and haloed in sunlight*. On the way to Denver he noted sagebrush and tumbleweed. He also thought he saw a buffalo, away off in the distance. He could not be sure, but he made a note of it anyway, since he knew this was a place where buffalo were supposed to be: *Defiant bull silhouetted against the blazing sky*. At Greeley he saw windmills, and put them down. If the track had been smoother, he would have drawn pictures.

Between trains in Cheyenne, he lugged the trunk from the station to a dry-goods store, where he bought a pair of pearl-handled revolvers and silver-studded holsters, the only items he had not been able to order through the mails. He was amazed by their weight. How were you supposed to walk straight with them hanging around your waist? He would have to practice in his room in Laramie.

That was the next stop after Cheyenne. When he stepped down onto Laramie's main street, he gave a little hop and stamped the dirt, to prove to himself he was truly there. He took a room upstairs from the Stardust Saloon, figuring he could gather material by listening through the floor. He was scarcely inside the door when he heard angry cries and the boom of a gunshot from down below. Immediately he pulled out his notebook and wrote a description. It was hard to keep his handwriting neat, the way his heart was thudding.

He also had trouble unlocking the trunk with his shaking fingers. He pulled out his gear and put it on, from high-heeled boots to Stetson hat, complete with lasso over his shoulder and the heavy six-shooters dangling from his hips. There was no mirror, which was just as well. His nerves could only take so much at one time. When he walked across the room he made a terrific noise, the spurs rattling, chaps creaking, fringes on his jacket swishing, guns clacking against the studs on his belt. He did not know how far he could carry all this weight, but it was high time to find out. He pushed his door open, peeked into the hallway, then eased down the stairs, clattering and creaking, onto the wooden sidewalk.

So far as he could tell, posing there in front of the saloon with the hat yanked down low over his eyes, nobody was paying much attention to him. That was good, he told himself. It meant he was blending in. He crossed his arms and leaned against a post, partly for effect, partly to balance the weight of the six-shooters. Now and again a passer-by would glance at him, make an odd face, and shuffle past. Sherwood was struck by how grubby everyone looked. The women's dresses appeared to be made of flour sacking, and their hairdos resembled the nests of large messy birds. The men were even shabbier. The leather of their boots was cracked, their jeans were caked with dirt, their hats might have been used for pillows. Watching them from beneath the clean brim of his own hat, he was also struck by the crookedness of their bodies, as if their skeletons had shattered and been glued back together imperfectly. Perhaps these were only town cowboys, seedier and shabbier than the ones he would meet out on the range.

Thinking about the range, he recalled that he would have to buy a horse and learn to ride. All along, this had been the most troubling part of his scheme, for he was terrified of animals. And his fear increased in proportion to the animal's size. Authors did not often remark on the hugeness of horses, but Sherwood knew from his observations in Cleveland that even ponies were several times larger than a man. The very heads of horses looked evil to him, like blunt spades or thick ax blades. He was fretting about this when a man galloped up, swung to the ground, and tethered his horse to the post where Sherwood was leaning.

Sherwood leapt back. The horse rolled its enormous eyeballs at him, as if calculating where to bite. Still backing, Sherwood passed the saloon and was halfway across the neighboring alley, when suddenly from the shadows there came a pitiful groan. His first impulse was to run, but his second was to see what artistic material might lie behind that groan. The artistic impulse won out. He crept into the alley, alarmed by the racket he was making. "Is anybody there?" he called hesitantly.

"Just barely," said a raspy voice. "But I won't be here long."

Peering into the gloom, Sherwood made out the shape of a man dressed in shabby cowboy gear and folded against a building with his legs spraddled flat on the ground. Light slanting from a window of the saloon illuminated his face, which was so crisscrossed with wrinkles it made Sherwood think of a railway map. The man's eyes were screwed shut. But as Sherwood hesitated, they blinked open and stared up at him, two bulbs the color of raw liver.

"I see by your outfit that you're a cowboy," the man rasped. "Thank God! You won't go off and leave a fellow here to die all by his lonesome in an alley."

Hearing himself addressed as a cowboy, Sherwood lost the ability to reason, and stood there transfixed. He bent toward the man and asked, "Are you injured?"

"Injured? I'm teetering on the brink of the grave. I'm shot through and through, bleeding like a stuck pig."

Only then did Sherwood notice the belt of white linen wrapped around the man's chest. There was a dark stain the size of a fifty-cent piece over his left pocket. Sherwood immediately sagged to the ground and collapsed against the wall beside the cowboy, not so much out of sympathy as out of faintness.

"I been shot nine times before," the man explained, "but this time it's my death wound."

Sherwood took off his Stetson and fanned himself. "Give me a second to recover and I'll run get help."

"It ain't no use," the cowboy muttered. "I'm done for. What I need is somebody to stick by me while I slip out of this sorry world. Aw, it's awful." He moaned, thumping his bare head against the planks of the wall.

"Really," Sherwood insisted, "it'll only take me a minute to get a doctor." He drew his legs inward as if to rise.

The man seized him by the wrist. "Don't leave me, pardner. I'm beyond doctoring. Stick by me and hear my dying confession, one cowboy to another."

The word *confession* set off bells in Sherwood's head. For the first time since entering the alley, he remembered his art. Quietly he withdrew the notebook from inside his fringed coat and spread it open across his knees.

"Oh," the cowboy moaned, letting go of the wrist, "I done so much wrong I don't know where to start."

Sherwood licked his pencil and held it poised above the page. "Why don't you start with an account of your various murders."

"I ain't ever been murdered before," the cowboy said.

"I mean the murders you *committed*."

"Aw, them. There's so many I can't remember them all."

"Then just tell me about the most exciting one." Sherwood printed on the top line, "THE DYING COWBOY," and immediately below, "Confessions while Cashing in His Chips."

The scratching of the pencil drew the man's bloodshot gaze, first to the notebook, and then to Sherwood's face. In an amazed voice, he said, "You writing this *down?*"

"Do you mind terribly?" said Sherwood.

"Naw, go on ahead." The man rolled his head away and screwed his eyes shut again. "And here I took you for a cowboy."

"Oh, I *am* a cowboy," Sherwood insisted. "A cowboy *author*."

"The world's got one of everything."

When the man kept silent for a minute, Sherwood prompted him: "You were going to describe your most exciting murders."

"Murders! Robberies! Snowslides and grizzly bears and Indians! Aw, the things I could tell!" He was cut short by a gurgling cough, which thumped his skull against the wall. "But I ain't got enough time left for that. I got just enough breath to plan my funeral."

"Couldn't you even tell me a tidbit about fighting Indians?"

"I want a coffin made out of cottonwood," the man declared. "With brass nails. Dress my corpse in a snow-white suit and put a five-gallon hat on my head and stuff a new deck of cards in my pocket. Lay gold pieces on my lids. Paint the outside of my box sky blue and let me have a few clouds on it." Suddenly his eyes peeled open and fixed on Sherwood. "You getting all this down?"

"Yes, of course," Sherwood stammered, jotting the last few instructions.

"All right. And I want six gamblers to carry the coffin and six pretty girls to walk along beside it holding that cloth they hang over it. What's that called?"

"A pall, I believe."

"Right. Make mine out of white linen. Get somebody to play a lazy march on the drums and fife while they're toting me to the graveyard. And have six cowboys ride alongside, picking guitars and singing me songs about the lone prairie and grazing buffalo and get-along dogies and like that. You with me?"

"Yes," said Sherwood, beginning a fresh page.

"And I want to be buried down in a green valley, I don't care how far you have to look to find one. I want grass and a creek and all kind of birds tweeting. Make sure the hole's too deep for the wolves to dig me up. Eight feet ought to do it. And before you dump in the dirt get a preacher to read some of the Good Book. There's one over to Cheyenne."

"A Bible?" Sherwood asked.

"A preacher. I reckon he's got a Bible. You may have to get the pretty girls over in Cheyenne, too." The man's voice was thinning out into a wheeze. "Have them pile roses over my box to cover up the sound of the dirt when they shovel it on me. Throw in a saddle, maybe, and a good bridle. And make sure my mamma knows about it before they plant me, in case she wants to come."

"Where is she?" Sherwood asked.

"Pittsburgh, last thing I heard."

Sherwood was still writing "Mamma—Pittsburgh" in his notebook when the man quit wheezing and slumped over onto the ground. For a moment Sherwood held his breath, listening. Then he gingerly prodded one of the outstretched legs with the dull end of his pencil. The body did not stir.

They'll think I did him in, thought Sherwood, scrambling to his feet. He glanced at the dark stain on the man's chest, then at his own gun, and a smothering sense of guilt came over him, as if he had actually done the shooting. He backed quickly from the alley, his gear jangling. No use fetching a doctor. Perhaps if he went straight to the sheriff, explained everything, they would let him off. No, no, they would pin it on him, throw him in jail, lynch him tomorrow morning. This was the West. You couldn't count on justice and good sense.

Sherwood trooped up and down the main street of Laramie, arguing with himself, oblivious to the horses and wagons and shuffling people that slid by him. Every time he passed the alley he peeped in, glimpsed the body, and shuddered. Finally he gathered his courage to go find the sheriff, anything to stop this whirlwind of fear. But on his next trip by the alley, the corpse was gone. Sherwood halted with a clatter and stared at the emptiness. In his mind he could see the stiff cowboy lying across the sheriff's desk, could see the posse gathering, could hear the horses approaching with their heavy hoofs and scorching breath. He stumbled in a fearful daze into the saloon, groping for the stairs. He was halfway up the first flight when a raspy voice from the bar made him turn his head. And there, leaning against the brass rail, still wrapped in the bandage, but laughing now and tipping an amber bottle to his lips, was the dead cowboy.

After a moment of paralyzing astonishment, Sherwood lunged on up the stairs, two steps at a time, not caring how much racket he made. In his room he tore off the guns, the lasso, the fringed coat, the hat, and flung them on the bed. He slapped his notebook down on the trunk and began furiously scribbling the opening page of his novel. In it the wounded cowboy would confess adventures that no mortal had ever lived through before, and at the end of the book, slumped against a wall in an alley, a grimace on his leathery face, Sherwood's hero would gracefully but surely die.

Sweet Betsy from Pike

[TRADITIONAL]

Have you ever heard tell of Sweet Betsy from Pike,
Who crossed the wide mountains with her lover Ike,
With two yoke of oxen, a large yellow dog,
A tall Shanghai rooster and an old spotted hog?

Saying, goodbye, Pike County,
Farewell for a while,
We'll come back again
When we've panned out our pile.

One evening quite early, they camped on the Platte,
'Twas near by the road on a green shady flat,
Where Betsy, quite tired, laid down to repose,
While with wonder Ike gazed on his Pike County rose.

They soon reached the desert, where Betsy gave out
And down in the sand she lay rolling about,
While Ike in great tears looked on in surprise,
Saying, "Betsy get up, you'll get sand in your eyes."

Sweet Betsy got up in a great deal of pain,
And declared she'd go back to Pike County again.
Then Ike heaved a sigh and they fondly embraced,
And she traveled along with his arm round her waist.

The Shanghai ran off and the cattle all died,
The last piece of bacon that morning was fried,
Poor Ike got discouraged, and Betsy got mad,
The dog wagged his tail and looked wonderfully sad.

One morning they climbed up a very high hill,
And with wonder looked down into old Placerville.
Ike shouted and said, as he cast his eyes down,
"Sweet Betsy, my darling, we've got to Hangtown."

Long Ike and Sweet Betsy attended a dance,
Where Ike wore a pair of his Pike County pants,
Sweet Betsy was covered with ribbons and rings,
Quoth Ike, "You're an angel, but where are your wings?"

A miner said, "Betsy, will you dance with me?"
"I will, old hoss, if you don't make too free.
But don't dance me hard. Do you want to know why?
Dog on ye, I'm chuck full of strong alkali."

Long Ike and Sweet Betsy got married, of course,
But Ike, getting jealous, obtained a divorce.
And Betsy, well satisfied, said with a shout,
"Goodbye, you big lummox, I'm glad you backed out."

Saying, goodbye, dear Isaac,
Farewell for a while.
But come back in time
To replenish my pile.

Wriggling her toes in the mud of the Mississippi, pretending she was a sycamore rooted there, Betsy looked westward over Missouri toward a dirty smudge on the horizon where she imagined California to be. Two thousand miles away, people said. The land between here and yonder was a blank in her mind, a great brown waste sprinkled with Indians and buffalo and tornadoes. Two thousand miles! Only by imagining that California was just over the hill, a blotch on the horizon, could she force herself to uproot from this place and leave Pike County behind.

"You ready, gingerbread?" said her husband, Ike. He had the wagon loaded and the four oxen yoked and he was standing on shore with the vacant look of a man whose mind was already four months west of here. She knew what he was thinking of just by the sag in his lips. Gold, gold, gold. Lately, that was the only wind blowing through his drafty head.

Betsy wriggled her toes one last time in the Mississippi goo. No telling when she would find any honest-to-goodness mud again, out there in the desert. Then she waded onto the bank, her skirt smacking wet against her knees, climbed onto the wagon seat, and said, "If you're waiting on me, you're backing up."

"Yahoo!" Ike gave the lead ox a flick on the rump with his bullwhip, and the wagon lurched into motion. The yellow hound trotted on ahead, nosing out the trail. The spotted hog, tied by a rope to the brake lever, scuffled along beside.

Betsy did not turn around to look at the homestead they were abandoning. It made her throat close up just thinking about the cabin, the herb garden, the patch of rhubarb and asparagus, the henhouse, the barn. To have seen all that dip and sway and disappear backward over the rim of the earth would have killed her. She looked ahead, toward the smudge on the horizon. California—where grown men staggered about with shiny rocks in their pockets, trains ran through holes in the mountains, volcanoes spouted fire, towns rose and fell overnight like blisters, Spaniards and Chinamen and Indians mixed in the streets with Americans—California, where any day offered up more craziness than a year in Missouri. And here we go carry our two buckets of dreams to that madhouse, thought Betsy.

She glared down at her wet feet, which peeped like twin piglets from beneath the hem of her skirt. No woman in Pike County had tinier feet. Betsy was skimpy all over, for that matter, everywhere except in her mind. "She might be a small package," Ike would tell visitors, "but so is a charge of blasting powder."

When her feet were dry, she brushed them clean and propped them on top of the Webster's dictionary.

"You mean to say we're going to haul *books* all the way over the mountains?" Ike had complained the night before when she was piling the Webster's, the Bible, the *Poetry Omnibus*, and the *Universal Classics* into the wagon.

"If they don't go, I don't go," Betsy had replied.

Ike had let her keep the books. Watching her load a bundle of baby clothes, he had only hoisted his eyebrows. "Sooner or later they'll come in handy," she told him.

"Sooner or later," he agreed.

Now he was marching up front with the oxen, singing for all he was worth, not thinking about babies or two thousand miles of travel, not a thought in the world except gold. Once in motion, she knew, he would not stop until he reached California. It was a sickness in his heart, a yen worse than gambling or drink. Otherwise he was a good enough man, better than most. You took what you could get, and Ike was what she had got. Thick in the shoulders and skull, kindly, gentle, with caterpillar eyebrows and stiff brown hair that stood up like broom straws and made him look eternally surprised, a boiled red face as round as a washpot, and a daydreamer's eyes, he was the pick of the men who had come wooing.

"If you'd stood in that river much longer," he called to

her, "you'd have sweetened the water all the way to New Orleans."

Betsy let a smile leak around the corners of her mouth. That man could think up flattering nonsense in his sleep. Rough words came so naturally to her own lips, she was amazed by the way he always came up with smooth ones. After four years of marriage it was still one of her favorite things about him.

"Just close your pretty peepers, honeybun," said Ike, "and when you open them we'll be in the gold fields."

She closed her eyes and calculated. Two thousand miles in four months, between the rains of April and the mountain snows of September. Seventeen miles a day. Two or three miles an hour, maybe less, maybe more. Traveling five hours on some days, twelve or fifteen on other days. When she opened her eyes, the wagon still rattled through Pike County.

One day ran into the next. Betsy rocked on the wagon seat, listening to the Shanghai rooster and three fat hens cluck from their cages back underneath the canvas. Weary in the legs, Ike crawled up beside her onto the seat and passed the time by scheming how they would spend their gold.

"By dog, we'll get us an umbrella," he boasted.

"Why not two," she said, playing along with him and hoping to raise his sights a little, "one for weekdays and one for Sunday?"

"Two it is," he agreed. "And new boots for both of us."

"Let's hire a cobbler to live on our estate—"

"Estate?" Ike put in uneasily.

"—on our estate—why not?—and we can have him make

us fresh boots every morning. He could make saddles, too, with silver bangles and carved leather. And what about the stables!"

Before she could fill up the stables with tame antelopes and mountain lions, Ike declared, "I reckon we might get us a pair of good horses for riding into town."

"A hundred horses," said Betsy, "and a dozen carriages! And why not a sailing ship, to go have a look at China?"

Traveling to foreign lands was a notion so far outside the ruts of his usual thinking, the mention of China made him quit spending his riches for almost nine miles. Betsy played the millionaire game to humor him, but wondered if they ever would earn a dollar from panning gold. Likely it was all hogwash, this gold business. Better stay in Pike County and raise corn than traipse out to California and hunt for specks of glitter.

Silence was such a rarity around Ike that she took advantage of it to dip into the *Universal Classics*, balancing the open dictionary across her lap where she could hunt up the words she did not know. Whenever she read, Ike scooted away from her on the seat, as if to allow more air for her brain.

And, oh! it was a weary long going! They followed the Missouri to Independence, where they joined with a dozen or so other wagons to begin the Oregon Trail. As they rolled along the Platte River, every side-path fed more travelers onto the route. Soon the train of wagons and horses and mules and men afoot stretched farther ahead and behind than Betsy could see. She wondered if anybody was left at home east of the Mississippi. The plains turned to hills, the hills to mountains, and up they straggled for day after day, the oxen snorting, Ike spending his millions, Betsy reading her books or pondering, until just beyond Devil's Gate they crossed the highest ridge and started down.

Most nights, in the glow beside the lantern, Ike would spread a grubby map on the dirt and ask her to read the names of the gold towns.

"Volcano," she read, "Angels Camp, Fiddletown, Growlersburg, Grizzly Flats, Rough and Ready, You Bet, Cherokee Flat, Yankee Jims, Fairplay, Hangtown." Time and again she recited the names, and each time Ike settled on a new destination.

"I like the sound of Growlersburg," he might say, or, "We ought to strike it rich in You Bet, don't you figure? 'Bet' sounds almost like 'Betsy,' " or, "Angels Camp's most likely the place for my angel."

To Betsy the gold towns all sounded equally wild and raw. And map or no map, they all seemed to her impossibly far away.

And, oh! it was a weary long going! Rumors of Indians swept along the straggling line of travelers, but no warriors ever showed themselves. At night, Betsy often lay awake among the bundles and clucking hens in the wagon bed, listening between Ike's snores to the fearful noises in the darkness. One moonless night, she woke from a light doze to hear a scratching on the canvas. She stopped breathing. Her mind filled with the image of Ike's broom-straw topknot hanging from the belt of some brave. Quietly lifting the gun, she aimed at the roof and blasted a warning shot. Outside there was a scurry of heavy feet, then silence. Ike sprang upright and pawed the air. It took her an hour to soothe him back to sleep. Next morning she patched the hole in the canvas.

At Fort Bridger they turned southwest onto the California Trail and rattled into the desert. If you opened your mouth for half a minute, the blowing sand would coat your tongue and sharpen your teeth. The drier it got, the more Betsy yearned to be home in Missouri. The yellow hound trotted off sniffing one day and never came back. The spotted hog broke its leg in a prairie dog hole and rotted before they could make three meals off him. The hens suffocated in the heat, and the Shanghai rooster pecked his way out and scurried off into a dust storm. By Salt Lake City you could have turned Betsy around with a blade of grass, but Ike trudged on west with a ravenous gleam showing beneath his droopy eyelids.

They drank their barrels dry, and had to begin sipping the alkali waters of the desert. Since leaving Pike County they had been passing graves beside the trail, but out in Utah Territory the markers grew thicker than sagebrush. The bones of oxen and horses that had fallen along the way reminded Betsy of driftwood along the Mississippi after spring rains. One of their own oxen died near Silver Zone Pass, a second at Humboldt Meadows. To lighten the wagon for the remaining yoke of oxen, they tossed overboard the spinning wheel, anvil, chicken cages, piece after piece of the goods they had taken four years to buy, until little was left except Ike's prospecting tools and Betsy's books and the baby clothes.

"I'd sooner go without shoes than give up my tools," said Ike.

"I'd sooner go stark naked than do without my books," Betsy countered.

They both looked at the bundle of baby things.

Ike scraped his jaw with a fistful of fingernails. For an instant his face glowed with a yen for something besides gold. "Might as well hang on to them," he said. "Such itty-bitty clothes can't weigh hardly anything at all."

"Light as a sack of feathers," Betsy agreed.

"Just like you," said Ike, putting his arms about her waist and lifting her off the seat.

They inched along the Carson River, up into the California mountains. Here was a country God must have overlooked, thought Betsy. Maybe He blinked, maybe He got tired, maybe He ran out of trees and grass and water before raising these mountains. At the top of the climb, in Carson Pass, Ike stopped to give the lathered oxen a rest. Sore of body and heart, Betsy hobbled over to have a look down the western slope, expecting to hate what she saw. But what she saw was a sweep of green, broken here and there by the blue streaks of rivers. Far out in the gulf of air, birds lolled and spun like black snowflakes. She blinked, and tears blurred her vision, and the weight of wonder sat her down on a yellow rock beside the trail. This was California? This humped green swoop of country? Nothing in her books had made her tremble so. Were there words enough in all the dictionary to describe it? She made a roof over her eyes with the palm of a hand and stared west, imagining the boom towns, the cities on the coast, beaches, ocean, islands, ships gliding away over the curve of earth.

She was still pinned to the rock, dazed and dumbfounded, when Ike drove the wagon up. "If I could paint pictures," he said, "I'd paint you sitting there on a great pile of silver and gold, and you shining brightest of all."

"Help me up, Isaac," she said, unable to move.

He lifted her in his arms, saying, "My sack of goose down, my little sack of pigeon feathers," and plumped her onto the seat, shoved the Webster's under her feet, gave the oxen a smack of the whip, and yelled, "Yahoo!" as they eased downhill into the country of madness and millionaires.

SCOTT RUSSELL SANDERS was born in Memphis, Tennessee, and grew up among tale-tellers on the backroads of Ohio. He attended Brown University and earned a Ph.D. from Cambridge University. His other books of fiction include *Wilderness Plots*, *Fetching the Dead*, *Wonders Hidden*, and *Terrarium*. Alone or in company he loves to sing folk songs, sometimes off-key but always with gusto. He teaches literature at Indiana University, in Bloomington, where he lives with his wife and two children.